Power Mage is a work of fiction. Characters, names, places, and events are either the product of the author's imagination or used fictitiously. Any similarity to real persons, living or dead, is purely coincidental.

Cover design by eBook Launch

Edited by Karen Bennett

Beta reader: Tanner Likins

Want to know when my next book is released? SIGN UP HERE.

HONDO JINX

POWER MAGE

1

His name was Brawley Hayes, and if you had seen him standing there, tall and wiry in a t-shirt, jeans, and cowboy boots, watching the Key West street performers as the sun melted into the horizon, you could never have guessed that twenty-four hours later, he would be the subject of an international manhunt that would change the world forever.

Brawley grinned as the skinny calico jumped back and forth through a golden hoop held by her trainer, a red-faced man in a battered top hat, Hawaiian shorts, and a baggy t-shirt that read *The Cat Wizard*.

"Good girl, Callie!" the Cat Wizard said, proving that he was better at training cats than naming them. He swept the top hat from his head and gestured toward a pair of ladders with a length of clothesline stretched between them.

Callie climbed the ladder, delighting the crowd.

That's when the trouble started.

Thirty feet away, a trio of assholes set to laughing like a pack of hyenas. One of them was all duded up in a shiny dress shirt and a pair of sunglasses pushed up into his peroxide-blond hair. Cupping hands around his dark goatee, he shouted at the Cat Wizard, jacking with him, trying to throw him off this game. "Hope she doesn't fall!"

The Cat Wizard glanced nervously in their direction but kept performing.

Brawley clenched his fists. During his years on the Professional Bull Riders circuit, he'd traveled all over. No matter where he went, he saw guys like this. Loud fuckers who hung in groups and started shit where shit had no business being started.

Sometimes, Brawley ended up knocking their teeth out.

But not tonight. Not here.

This wasn't some backcountry honky-tonk, where men understood that words had consequences. This was Key West, a nice place. And he wasn't here to fight.

Besides, according to the doctors who had rebuilt his neck, one good smack—like say, a haymaker from that thick bastard next to Blondie—might pop the vertebral pin, slice the main artery, and bye-bye Brawley.

He'd been restless ever since getting out of the hospital. Restless and wracked by weird dreams of swaying palms, street performers, and a brightly painted sign that read *Welcome to Mallory Square, the World Famous Sunset Celebration!*

Which was strange, since he had never even heard of this place.

Then he'd found out it was real. All of it. The town, the celebration, even the damned sign. That very day, he'd left the ranch and headed east, driven by curiosity like a tumbleweed before a storm.

This place had drawn Brawley to it, and he wanted to know why. But he was pretty sure he hadn't been summoned across sixteen hundred miles merely to toss knuckles with these assholes.

So he did his best to ignore them and watch the show.

Callie was quite a cat. All these people, all this noise—hell, the next act over, some guy was juggling torches atop a ten-foot unicycle—but Callie was walking back and forth across the tightrope as calmly as she might cross the floor of a familiar barn.

That was poise, a trait Brawley held in high regard.

He decided to drop a five in the tip bucket.

Then Callie flew away.

The cat didn't jump. She just whipped away through the air, screaming with fear and zooming over the tourists like a cat riding an invisible flying carpet.

What the hell?

The Cat Wizard raced after her. The crowd followed, crying out with confusion.

A hundred feet from shore, Callie hovered in midair above the ocean.

Brawley shouldered his way to the water's edge and heard the Cat Wizard pleading with the trio of assholes.

"Pay up next time, Beastie," the blond-haired guy said.

Before Brawley could even wonder about that, Callie dropped into the water.

People screamed, staring in horror as the cat struggled.

At this distance, Callie's head was nothing but a colorful dot in the water, there and gone and there again, the cat obviously struggling to stay afloat in the choppy bay.

Brawley glanced around for a boat or anything he could use to save her, but there was nothing close enough to make a difference.

He considered kicking off his boots and jumping in, but his gut said he'd never reach her in time. And life had taught Brawley to trust his gut.

Come on, Callie. Come on, girl.

The cat was making no progress toward the shoreline despite her flailing.

3

"Oh my gawd, she's gonna drown!" a woman screamed.

Brawley's vision sharpened as it sometimes did when his adrenaline kicked in. Suddenly, he could see the struggling cat just as clearly as if he was looking through the Leupold gold ring atop his .308.

Callie spat and screamed, her eyes huge with terror. Then her head went under again.

Brawley reached out, wanting with every fiber of his being to do something, *anything*, to save the animal.

She broke the surface again, eyes rolling with horror.

Strange pressure was building in Brawley's head. A line of fire burned up the back of his neck, making him wonder if he had reinjured it somehow.

He blocked this out, focusing on the cat. The roar of the crowd faded to a dull murmur, and the world went almost silent just like it used to when he was riding, back before Aftershock had taken it all away.

Come on, Callie. Fight, girl. Swim.

But the cat disappeared again—and stayed under this time.

Brawley was seized by a sense of powerful anticipation, as if life had rushed sharply in one direction with the whoosh of a drawn-back whip, and now he was waiting for the sharp crack of the return stroke.

Brawley's heart hammered like bull hooves in his chest. Heat and pressure filled his skull, which felt like a volcano about to erupt.

Crouching down, he reached out with both arms.

Callie resurfaced with a pitiful yowl.

Then, suddenly, Brawley could *feel* the cat.

He could feel her struggling. Not in his hands but in some other hands, the hands of his imagination, it seemed.

He imagined using those hands to hoist the cat to safety, and the crowd cried out, pointing as Callie lifted into the air.

Which wasn't possible. But given the circumstances, Brawley didn't give a shit about what was or wasn't possible. In his view of things, once you set your mind on something, you stuck to it and didn't quit till the thing was finished. Right now, he only cared about saving the cat. Possibility be damned.

"That's it, girl," he said, and concentrated on pulling her toward land. "I got you."

Callie drifted toward him through the air, swaying back and forth. It was like invisible hands were holding her under the arms. "Come on, pretty girl."

Brawley felt foolish then, realizing he'd been talking out loud and gesturing with his arms like a lunatic.

People gawked.

Oh well. Let them stare.

He stayed focused on Callie. At last her bony body came into his hands—his *real* hands this time—and he pulled the wet, trembling cat to his chest.

Which Callie promptly scratched the shit out of, squealing like someone had stomped her tail.

Lines of fire zipped across his flesh as the panicked feline sprang free and raced across the pavement to the Cat Wizard, who scooped her into his arms and sobbed with relief.

Brawley's white t-shirt was a bloody, tattered mess, and the scratches burned like hell, but he burst into loud laughter anyway.

He'd done it. It shouldn't have even been possible, but he had saved the cat.

Everyone was staring at him now.

Some smiled.

A few applauded, having somehow convinced themselves that this had been a trick and that Brawley was a performer, part of the show.

Other folks weren't so enthusiastic. They backed away, eyes bulging, making the sign of the cross or pulling kids close as they hustled off.

Then everything went sideways.

All the strength drained out of Brawley. He stumbled, and the world around him lurched and spun like he was riding a rank bull. The cobblestones tilted, and he almost dropped.

Only his superhuman balance, which he had honed over years and years of training and competition, saved him. He came to again, still on his feet, and the spinning slowed.

But he was sick as hell and had a wall-banger of a headache. And he was thirstier than he'd ever been in his life, which was saying something, coming from a guy who'd grown up in West Texas.

He needed a drink. Pronto.

"Thank you, mister," the Cat Wizard said, appearing with Callie in his arms and tears streaming down his stubbled cheeks. "Thank you for saving my girl. Bless you."

Then a middle-aged woman was sticking a phone in Brawley's face. "Most amazing thing I've ever seen! How in the world did you do that?"

"Excuse me, ma'am," Brawley said, "but I really need a drink."

"Who *are* you?" the woman exclaimed.

Brawley didn't feel like hanging around, but he had been raised to be polite, especially to women, and that went double for women who happened to be older than him. Also, his time on the circuit had conditioned him to answer questions and pause for photos even after getting thrown or stomped.

He cleared his parched throat and said, "My name is—"

And then the woman's phone snapped in half and dropped to the cobblestones in a rain of twisted metal and shattered screen bits.

The woman reared back like a spooked horse, knifing the air with terrified shrieks.

Brawley could only stand and stare, wondering just what the hell kind of otherworldly hornet's nest he had kicked coming here.

Then someone grabbed him by the arm and started dragging him away through the crowd.

"Come with me now," the girl beside him growled, "or you'll get us both killed."

2

Looking down, Brawley couldn't believe his eyes.

Hustling him through the crowd was a tiny woman who looked like a cross between a Victoria's Secret model and a rodeo clown.

Even in his current state, even at a glance, Brawley could see that she was drop-dead gorgeous—despite her studded dog collar, glittering nose ring, and crazy hair, which was long and purple, except for where she'd shaved one side of her head to stubble. She wore combat boots, camouflage cut-offs, a plaid flannel knotted around her waist, fingerless gloves, and a skin-tight tank top emblazoned with an anarchy symbol and crisscrossed with little slashes that exposed lines of tanned flesh.

She was of an age with Brawley, somewhere in her early twenties, and couldn't have been more than five-three beneath that heap of purple locks. She was slender and toned with great collarbones and amazing curves that jiggled hypnotically as she marched him away from whatever the hell had just happened back there.

After his first couple of years on the circuit, Brawley had

largely avoided the inevitable army of dolled-up groupies who turned up in every town to stalk the bull riders. Most of the buckle bunnies were beautiful, but they tended to be loud and showy, and their makeup, short-shorts, and pushup bras felt like a trap to Brawley.

He preferred *real* women. Mostly country girls, who were pretty without the fuss and who could sit a horse, handle a rifle, gut a fish, or throw together a Sunday dinner for twelve on short notice.

This girl was about as far from his type as he could imagine but looking at her was like getting whacked right between the eyes with a ball-peen hammer. She was next-level gorgeous, purple faux hawk and crazy clothes be damned.

"I love cats, too, but what the actual fuck were you thinking?" she snarled. "Do you have a death wish or are you just a moron?"

Before he could answer, an angry voice called out behind them, "Stop running, Nina. We want to talk to your boyfriend."

"Go fuck yourselves!" Nina replied, and hauled Brawley into an alley packed with tourists.

Brawley slammed on the brakes. If those assholes wanted trouble, he'd give them all the trouble they could handle and then some.

But when he tried to jerk his arm free, he couldn't break Nina's grip.

And that was curious. Ponderously curious.

Brawley was 6'2" in his sock feet and broad across the shoulders, 170 pounds of whipcord muscle hardened by riding bulls and handling everything his hardscrabble ranch life threw his way, from roping cattle to mending fences to putting up hay.

And yet this angry little punk rocker, who probably

tipped the scales a few ounces either side of a hundred pounds, hauled him down the alley like a mother bear dragging her cub by the ear.

That's when Brawley realized just how weak he was. Whatever happened back there had sure enough knocked the hell out of him.

His legs wobbled, twitching with fatigue. Explosions of pain popped like fireworks in his skull, blurring his vision. His throat was drier than a desert road.

"You're a piece of work, cowboy," Nina said as they left the alley and cut across the street. A slow-moving herd of people wearing cruise ship badges packed the sidewalk. Nina and Brawley wove through them, hurried around a corner, and hung a quick left into another alley.

At the other end, Nina mounted a pink moped covered in stickers and slapped the seat behind her. "Can you ride?"

The world reeled, crazier than a funhouse mirror. But Nina's question brought Brawley around. People had been asking him that same question since he'd fallen off his first sheep back in his mutton-busting days. And Brawley told her the same thing he told people every time somebody asked, no matter how bad he was hurting. "I can ride."

He squeezed in behind her, barely fitting on the seat, and folded up his long legs. He grabbed her tiny waist with his big calloused hands, wrapping his fingers across her hip bones and onto her taut abdomen, one finger sliding into the slit fabric and pressing into her warm flesh.

Nina zipped down the street, whipping away from the shouts of the assholes, who had finally made it to the end of the alley.

Brawley focused on not falling off the bike. He was dead tired and dizzy. His head roared with pain, and he felt like puking.

It was like being drunk and hungover all at the same time.

But Nina's toned body still felt good. Her piled-up hair was a purple cushion beneath his chin. He breathed in her smell, an intoxicating blend of fresh ocean air, sweet pineapple, and Caribbean flowers.

"Where are you staying?" Nina shouted over her shoulder.

"Nowhere yet."

Five minutes later, they pulled onto Fleming Street and stopped in front of a sign that read Eden House.

Two steps led to a deep, shady porch full of rockers. A black cat sat in one of the rockers, blinking lazily. A wide set of double doors opened onto a hotel lobby. A skinny guy with a beard stood behind the counter, leafing through a magazine.

"Get a room," Nina said. "You're falling apart. Meet me at Blue Heaven at midnight."

"Huh?" Brawley wasn't normally an idiot, but his head felt like a bull had stomped it.

"Go," Nina said, peeling his hands from her flat stomach and pointing toward the double doors of the inn. "Remember: Blue Heaven at midnight. You owe me pie, cowboy!"

Then, without so much as flipping him the bird, the feisty beauty zipped away on her pink moped.

Brawley staggered inside.

The bearded man behind the counter looked up from his magazine and frowned. "You don't look so hot. Do you need medical assistance?"

Brawley shook his head. "I'll be all right," he said, sticking to one of the life mottoes his grandmother had hammered into him since birth: *never complain, never explain*. "What I need is something to drink."

The man reached back and opened a mini-fridge and pulled out a can of Bud beaded with condensation. "Complimentary with check-in. You are checking in, right?"

"Yeah, sure." Brawley popped the can and took a long pull of the good, cold beer. Two more gulps and it was finished.

"Thank you, sir," Brawley said, setting the empty on the counter with a hollow clink. "You got any more of those? I'm so thirsty, my throat thinks my mouth's sewn shut."

A grin split the guy's beard. "Buck a piece. How many would you like?"

Brawley shoved a hand in his hip pocket, came out with a five, and slapped it on the counter.

"You really are thirsty."

"Yes, sir."

The man took the money and set a six-pack on the counter. "Volume discount."

Brawley nodded thanks and went through the sixer, chugging one after another. He knew he must look a sight, standing there knocking back beer after beer, but he was too thirsty to give a damn.

The man watched, grinning. "Better?"

Brawley muffled a belch. "Yes, sir. Somewhat." Chugging the beers had taken the edge off his thirst, and he had a little buzz going.

"There's water over there," the man said, pointing across the lobby to a bank of glass decanters with slices of fruit floating in the water.

Brawley thanked him and crossed the room and pounded what felt like a gallon of water. That finally quenched the fire in his throat, but his muscles were twitching like crazy, and one of his eyelids had developed a tic. He staggered back to the counter. "What's your cheapest room?"

"234 a night, plus tax."

Brawley whistled. "234 a night? What's it come with, whores and whiskey?"

The man grinned. "I'm afraid not, sir. Just the beer you already drank."

Brawley shrugged and pulled out his billfold. "I'll take it." Noticing the rack of pamphlets, he snagged a city map.

"If you need help finding anything, let me know."

"Actually," Brawley said, slipping the map into his back pocket, "you ever heard of Blue Heaven?"

The man set the paperwork on the counter and showed him where to sign. "Blue Heaven's on Petronia Street. Twenty-minute walk from here. Very popular. If you like history, eat inside and your waitress will tell about how the place used to be a brothel. Or if you favor atmosphere, eat outside. It's the best in town."

Brawley thanked him and paid in cash.

Making change, the man said, "We have free parking on the side. You want to put down a plate number?"

Brawley shook his head. He'd parked the RV by a Publix on the far side of the island, having heard that the only thing worse than driving in Key West was trying to park. And that was with a car. No way was he driving the Winnebago into Old Towne.

"How about a cell phone number?"

"Don't have one." Brawley didn't bother explaining that he hated computers, microphones, and even the walkie-talkies they used on the ranch. Electronics made his brain buzz, and often as not went on the fix when he handled them.

They finished up the paperwork, and the man said, "Come with me, sir, and I'll show you to your room."

When they reached the stairs, the man offered to carry Brawley's rucksack.

Brawley said thanks but no thanks, thinking *to hell with that.*

"Need a hand up the stairs?" the man asked.

Brawley shook his head and grabbed the railing. Cursing

this strange weakness, he dug deep and hauled himself to the top.

They crossed a balcony overlooking a pool where people were swimming and drinking and laughing, Jimmy Buffet playing on the speakers. Some of the women looked pretty good in their bikinis, but Brawley felt so lousy, he couldn't be bothered to take a second glance.

The man unlocked the door and handed Brawley the key. "Enjoy your stay," the man said. "If you go to Blue Heaven, don't miss their key lime pie. It's to die for."

You owe me pie, cowboy.

Brawley asked for an eleven o'clock wakeup call. Then he went into the room and closed the door and turned the lock.

He dropped his ruck and fell into bed without bothering to turn down the covers or take off his boots. He figured he'd lay there for just a second, then grab a shower and maybe catch some shuteye before going back out to meet Nina.

This had been the craziest damned day ever.

How had that cat gone flying through the air? It seemed like the assholes had done it, like they were shaking down the Cat Wizard.

How had Brawley managed to pull Callie out of the water?

And how had that woman's phone snapped in half like that?

Crazy, all of it. Impossible. Like a strange dream.

Though the burning scratches beneath his tattered shirt begged to differ.

Nina hadn't seemed surprised. Just pissed that Brawley had saved the cat. Did that mean…

The phone rang.

Brawley jolted up out of bed.

For an instant, he was confused.

Slices of illumination fell through the louvered shutters,

striping the floor of the otherwise darkened room. He could hear music and laughter out by the pool, softer now.

The phone rang again.

He fumbled around the nightstand and picked up the receiver just as the phone rang a third time. It was a woman from the front desk, delivering the wakeup call.

Brawley didn't even remember shutting his eyes. Could it be eleven already?

He thanked her and hung up and turned on some lights. He pulled off his boots, stripped down, and took a hot shower.

His headache and fatigue were gone. The dizziness and nausea, too. He felt fine. Better than fine, in fact. He felt good. Just a little thirsty.

By the time he left the room and stepped into that beautiful, tropical night, he had a plan. Go meet Nina, buy her pie, and get the fuck out of Dodge the next morning. Head back to Texas and sell the RV. With his touring days behind him, Brawley needed cash a lot more than he needed a camper. Then he'd figure out what to do with the rest of his life.

Just settle into cowboying, probably. He loved the life. Only problem was he got bored sometimes. Not when he was working but the times in between, when he'd ride into town. When he got bored, he got stupid. And when he got stupid, he got into trouble.

The night was warm and peaceful beneath a fat moon blurry with tropical haze. Two girls coasted by on bicycles, soft laughter trailing behind them. Otherwise, Fleming was quiet and empty, save for cats, which peeked and peered from the plentiful porches and palms lining the street.

As Brawley drew close to the library, a hulking figure rose up within the shadowy foliage beside the front steps and lumbered halfway into the light. Despite the Florida heat, the man wore a raggedy winter jacket smudged with filth. His tangled beard was streaked in dark matter, blood or tobacco juice.

The man's bulging eyes gleamed in the light. He raised an arm and pointed a gnarled finger at Brawley.

Brawley raised one hand reflexively to his brow, forgetting for the thousandth time that he wasn't wearing his cowboy hat. He hadn't worn it since breaking his neck. And he'd vowed to never wear it again until he climbed back onto a bull. Which, according to doctors, would be around the same time that pigs flew to hell and went ice skating.

But then the big crazy-looking bastard started jabbering, and Brawley forgot all about his hat or bull riding or the way doctors could look you in the eyes, tell you matter-of-factly that everything you loved was gone forever, wish you a good day, and vanish from your life, carrying a clipboard under one arm and all of your hopes and dreams under the other.

"Thunder rider," the man said, jabbing his finger in Brawley's direction. "Lightning bringer. The despised messiah." He clapped his grimy hands together, the sound sharp and loud on this deserted street. "Now the two-headed wolf, order and chaos, fights itself, both jaws setting upon the same throat."

Brawley noticed with a twitch of unease that the man's beard wasn't stained after all. It was full of bugs. Whole rivers of them streaming up and down the hairs.

It was a strange thing, getting goosebumps in the tropics.

Brawley started walking again. He wasn't in the habit of turning his back on people, but this guy was nuttier than a squirrel turd.

"Seven, seven, seven," the man called after Brawley. "Seven minds, seven wives, seven strands. Seek the past to know the future. Beware the albino tiger!"

3

As Brawley approached the wide gate to Blue Heaven, a voice called, "Hey cowboy!" and a heavily stickered pink moped whooshed past.

Nina parked and came down the sidewalk looking super hot in combat boots, white short-shorts, and a star-spangled bikini top that showed off the tanned perfection of her flat abs, shapely breasts, and sexy collar bones. She strutted toward him with a cocky grin, her purple hair bristling like the comb of a fighting rooster.

"You survived," Nina said, her voice full of laughter.

"I'm hard to kill."

"Good," Nina said, slipping her slender arm through his and heading toward the wide gate of Blue Heaven, "because you owe me pie."

Even at midnight, there was a line, but Nina called to the hostess, who gestured for them to skip the wait and come inside.

Arm-in-arm, they followed the brick walkway past tables packed with people eating and drinking and entered a court-yard with more tables and a live band playing reggae on a canopied stage. A bunch of cats and chickens wandered the cobbles, going table to table and somehow managing to live in peace as they scavenged food and attention.

Nina bumped him with her hip. "You buying me drinks, too?"

"Least I can do," he said, and nodded toward the bar. "Let's go."

They found stools at the end of the outdoor bar.

The bartender, a heavyset woman with gray hair and a great smile, came over and called Nina by name. "What are we drinking?"

"Something sweet and strong," Nina said. "And your biggest slice of key lime pie, please."

The bartender nodded and turned to Brawley. "How about you, slim? What's your poison?"

Brawley ordered his go-to meal: a beer, a coke, and a bacon cheeseburger, rare, with fries on the side.

When the bartender left, Brawley turned to Nina. She sat close to him, one tanned leg flopped casually against his thigh.

She looked fantastic in that bikini top. Vibrant and healthy. Firm yet feminine. Her collarbones drew his eyes, the shadowed hollows within their graceful curves somehow suggestive and intimate.

"Hey cowboy," she said, "my badass Skrillex haircut is up here."

Brawley managed to drag his eyes, kicking and screaming, from her scantily clad perfection.

Grinning, Nina gave him a shove. "I thought cowboys were supposed to be gentlemen."

"Oh, I'm a gentleman," he said, "but that doesn't mean I'm blind."

Nina rolled her eyes. She was wearing dark eyeliner that made her eyes seem even brighter.

One green eye, one bright blue, Brawley noticed.

"Are those your real eye colors, or are you wearing contacts?"

"Wow," Nina said, "you're straightforward."

"Never saw much percentage in beating around the bush."

"They're real," Nina said. "It's called heterochromia."

"I had a dog with two different colored eyes."

"Wow," Nina said again, "you're a sweet talker, too."

"He was a good dog, if that makes a difference."

Nina laughed. She really was very pretty. A tiny diamond stud twinkled on the side of her nose.

The bartender brought their drinks. "Food will be up soon."

"Be warned," Nina said, after the bartender had left again. "We're on island time. In Key West, 'soon' means sometime before taxes are due. What's your name, anyway?" She held out her hand to shake. "I'm Nina."

Her hand felt small and soft. Then again, most people's hands felt small and soft to Brawley. Even for his height, he had huge hands—*bear paws,* his dad called them—and ranch work and riding had hardened them with callouses. "I'm Brawley."

"Brawley?" Nina laughed. "Is that even a name?"

"I sure hope so. It's the only one I got."

"Well then, it's nice to meet you, Brawley. A lot nicer than our first meeting at Mallory Square."

"About that," he said. "What the hell happened there?"

"What happened?" She made a face. "Your dumb ass saved a cat and got me in trouble, that's what happened."

"Got you in trouble?"

Nina nodded. "Nothing I can't handle but still a pain in my sweet ass." She leaned closer and whispered, "The asshole with the blond hair, that was Junior Dutchman."

"You say that like it's a bad thing."

"It is," she said. "Junior is the son of Mr. Dutchman."

"Don't just sit there staring at me, sweetheart. The only Dutchman I know is RVs."

"Mr. Dutchman runs the local psi mob."

"Mob? You mean mafia?"

Nina leaned back, narrowing her eyes and studying his face.

Reading her expression, Brawley headed her off at the pass. "Yeah, I'm being serious. I have no clue what you're talking about."

Nina lifted her drink and took a slow sip, still eyeing him and looking thoughtful. "No shit," she said, sounding incredulous. "You're a virgin."

Brawley snorted. "Not hardly."

"That little stunt with the cat," Nina said. "That was your first time, wasn't it? But I still don't understand why you were so rocked. I mean you had to know it was coming soon. What are you, twenty-four, twenty-five?"

"Twenty-three," he said, not bothering to add that on a rainy day, he felt eighty-three, thanks to all the injuries he'd sustained over the years. Luckily, they didn't get many rainy days in West Texas.

"Didn't your parents give you the talk?"

He shook his head. "My folks are country as a clambake, so they didn't talk about that stuff. But you grow up on a farm, you figure out the birds and the bees pretty quick."

"Not the birds and the bees, wiseass," Nina said. She still seemed to think he was messing with her. "Psionics. The do's and don'ts, the hangover, all that."

He shook his head and took a long pull off the beer.

Psionics?

He'd heard the word but couldn't remember what it meant. "What are psionics?"

"Psionic powers," Nina said, keeping her voice low.

"You're Unbound, like me, so in our case, that means telekinetic powers."

"Telekinetic powers," he said, drawing it out. "If you'd told me that yesterday, I would've thought you were loopier than a cross-eyed cowboy."

"I guess levitating a cat with telekinetic force opened your mind to the possibility?" Nina said.

Brawley nodded. "I'd be dumber than hell to scoff at this point."

"Seriously, though, your parents mentioned none of this?"

He shook his head.

"Nothing?"

"Not. A. Thing." He polished off his beer, pushed the bottle forward, and caught the bartender's eye.

She nodded, flashed that pretty smile, and started their way.

He asked Nina if she wanted another.

"Sure, thanks." She was rolling the little purple umbrella back and forth between her thumb and forefinger, making it spin.

Watching her, it occurred to Brawley that the little umbrella was the same shade of purple as her hair.

"You never saw either of them use their abilities?" she asked.

He laughed, imagining his parents having telekinetic powers. Sure would've made putting up hay easier. But then something occurred to him. "These powers, are you saying they're inherited?"

"Yeah."

Suddenly things made sense.

Before Brawley could say anything, the bartender brought his beer. Then she went off to make another girly drink for Nina.

"I'm an orphan," he said. "My father died before I was

born. My mother died shortly thereafter. Never really thought about it much, honestly. My folks adopted me when I was a newborn. They've always been Mom and Dad to me."

Something in Nina's face softened then. She reached out and laid her hand on his. "I'm sorry, Brawley," she said, and gave his hand a squeeze.

"Hell, don't be. Mom and Dad are great. And the world never saw a better woman than my Grandma Hayes, God rest her soul. I didn't miss out on anything."

"Except the talk," Nina said. She kept her hand on his, even though the moment had passed. Brawley liked the feel of it. "So, when you woke up this morning, you thought telekinesis was just in comic books and movies?"

He nodded. "Pretty much."

She shook her head and knocked back the rest of her drink just in time to thank the bartender, who brought her another. Nina dropped the cherry from the first on top of the second.

When the bartender left, Nina said, "Today must've been one heck of a shock for you."

"Yeah, it sucker punched me pretty good," he said. He felt strange. According to this woman, he had supernatural abilities, which was so weird that he should've been reeling, but for some reason, he wasn't. It was almost as if a part of him had known about this all along and had been waiting for him to catch up. "Telekinetic powers."

She nodded, fishing both cherries from her drink. "Pretty cool, huh?"

He took another drink. "And you have powers, too?"

Nina grinned. "I sure do. Want to see a trick?"

He nodded.

"I'm talented," Nina said with a mischievous smile. She popped both cherries into her mouth, started chewing, and held up one finger in a *wait-and-see* gesture.

Nina rolled her eyes upward with concentration, half smiling as she moved the cherries inside her pretty mouth. Her tongue slid back and forth inside her cheek.

She really was gorgeous. So gorgeous that even though Brawley was sitting there waiting for a telekinetic display, he was completely distracted by her full lips, long lashes, and big, mismatched eyes.

"Ha," Nina said triumphantly. Beaming, she pulled the cherry stems from her mouth. She'd swallowed the fruit and tied the stems in a knot with her tongue. "How's that for talent?"

"You call that a trick?" a sultry voice said from behind them.

"Oh shit," Nina said, without even turning around. "I didn't do anything, Remi."

A heavily tattooed brunette holding a Corona stepped into view, wearing black leather pants and a tight black tank top. She looked Brawley up and down and gave him a cocky smile.

Nina leaned into Brawley, frowning.

Remi simmered with confidence. She was undeniably, jaw-droppingly hot but also looked incredibly dangerous.

Her A+ rack strained against the thin fabric of her tight, black tank top, and her impressive muscles rippled, bringing to life the countless tattoos covering her body. There was something feral about her bright white teeth, dark irises, and the powerful grace with which she moved, and yet her face was strikingly beautiful in the classic sense, the type of beauty you see only once or twice in your life.

She was a study in contrasts, a bad girl with breeding, like a top model with royal blood who had given it all up to win a world title in MMA while shooting gonzo porn in her free time.

Remi sat down, putting an arm around Nina's shoulders

and pushing halfway onto her stool. "That wasn't a trick," she said, grinning at Brawley. "This is a trick."

Remi slid the bottle of corona down the front of her shirt and pulled her hands away. Her full, round breasts trapped the bottle between them.

Brawley couldn't help but stare as drops of condensation rolled off the bottle and trickled down Remi's firm boobs like beads of sweat.

"Incredible, aren't they?" Remi said, and gave her tits a squeeze. "But they're not my trick. This is."

Nina groaned.

Brawley slipped a comforting arm around her tiny waist but couldn't look away as Remi squeezed her boobs, flexing and relaxing, flexing and relaxing. Each repetition worked the bottle up and up until its tip reached her bright red lips, which slid over the bottle and sucked.

Lowering her head, Remi deep-throated the longneck. Then she tilted her head back, and the bottle popped free of her mesmerizing breasts.

The bottle sunk deeper until only a few inches jutted from her mouth. The rest bulged in her pretty throat. Her lips gripped the bottle's girth as she swallowed greedily, chugging beer. Foam drained from the corners of her mouth and ran down her throat and over her breasts, wetting the tight black fabric.

Still eyeing Brawley seductively, Remi gulped down the beer. Then she pulled the bottle from her mouth, wiped one muscular, heavily inked forearm across her wet, sexy mouth, burped, and threw back her head with rich laughter.

"Wow," Brawley said. "That was quite a show."

"I'm not done yet, handsome," Remi said.

"Don't, Remi," Nina said. "Seriously."

Remi shoved the bottle back into her mouth and—*crunch*—bit the longneck clean off. Then she started chewing.

Brawley couldn't believe his eyes. He'd seen a guy once in a honky-tonk chew a piece of glass about the size of your thumbnail. But Remi had bitten off the entire longneck, and he could hear the shards snapping as her jaws worked. "What the hell are you doing, girl?"

Remi laughed again, and Brawley glimpsed a mouthful of glass and blood.

He grabbed Remi's arm. It was smooth and hard with muscle, like a python. "Spit that shit out," he said. "You're cutting yourself."

Remi pulled her arm free then took Nina's drink, flicked the umbrella over one shoulder, and threw back the sweet-but-strong concoction. She swished the liquid for a few seconds and gulped it down.

Brawley winced. "That is not good for you."

Remi laughed and stuck out her tongue.

Brawley was no stranger to trauma, but he winced at the sight. Remi's tongue was all cut to hell and bleeding like crazy.

Only then it wasn't…

Remi was watching him intently. Watching him watching her.

And he couldn't stop staring. At her tongue, specifically. Because as he watched, the bleeding slowed and stopped. The terrible gashes shrunk and closed.

"You want to kiss it and make it better, lover boy?" Remi asked.

Brawley stared for a moment, second-guessing his eyes. "It's already better."

Remi swept his beer off the bar and chugged the rest. "You want to kiss it anyway?"

Nina slid off her stool and tugged Brawley's hand. "Let's go."

"All right," he said, pulling out his billfold.

"Pie and a burger," the bartender said, coming toward them with his meal and the biggest damn piece of pie he'd ever seen. The meringue alone was tall as a ten-gallon hat.

He tugged Nina's hand. "Your pie."

"I'm not hungry anymore."

"Don't worry, sweetie," Remi said, pulling the pie toward her. "I'll eat it all up for you."

4

"That sucks," Nina said as they left Blue Heaven. "I really wanted pie."

"We'll get you some," Brawley said. "There are signs for it everywhere."

Nina shook her head. "I lost my appetite. Let's go back to my place and talk."

"Sounds good. I got about a million questions."

"Go figure," Nina groaned. "Remi parked right next to me."

Nina's moped looked small and silly beside the huge, black Harley.

"What happened back there?" Brawley asked.

"Remi's a pain in the ass, that's what happened. We have history. She fucks with me every time I see her."

"I'm talking about the bottle. Her tongue was all cut to hell, then…"

Nina straddled the moped. "She's a Carnal."

Brawley got on behind her and wrapped his hands around her tiny waist. Once again, her hair brushed the underside of his chin and the good smell of her filled his nostrils. "The Carnals. Sounds like a biker gang."

Nina laughed. "Nope. Though Remi actually was raised by bikers."

"I believe it. She seems like a tough chick."

"The toughest," Nina said, pulling away from the curb. "Where do I start? There's so much to explain. I've never met a clueless twenty-three-year-old virgin."

"Just give it to me fast and hard, down and dirty, and we'll figure out the finer points as we go along."

"You're my kind of man, cowboy," Nina said. "Okay, so there are seven orders of psi mages, each built around a specific strand of psionic power. You and I are telekinetic, so we're force mages. That means we're in the Order of the Unbound. Well, I am. You'll have to register."

Brawley didn't like the sound of that. In his experience, most people were okay, one-on-one, but groups brought out the worst in them. And that went double for groups that required registration.

"Force mages include telekinetics, pyrokinetics, cryokinetics, electrokinetics, the list goes on and on. Bottom line, we reject the laws of physics and rewrite the rules. Hence 'The Unbound.'"

"All right," he said, and felt another little hiccup of reflexive incredulity, which he immediately booted. Second-guessing things at this point, after what he'd seen and experienced, would be stupid. Now was the time to learn the lay of this strange, new land. "What about the Carnals?"

"Carnals are flesh mages. They're biokinetics. They manipulate organic structures all the way down to the cellular level. So they're all super hot and strong and fast and a bunch of other stuff. They also tend to be a huge pain in the ass, as you probably noticed. Did I mention that I *love* pie?"

"Flesh mages," Brawley said thoughtfully. "So, Remi healed her tongue just like that?"

"Just like that," Nina said. "Carnals regenerate. Must be nice, huh?"

You're not kidding, Brawley thought. Over the years, he'd been thrown, stomped, butted, hooked, plowed over, and tossed. Before breaking his neck, he'd broken both hands, both collarbones, his nose, half his ribs, several teeth, and his sternum. He'd racked up more concussions than an NFL team, dislocated his shoulders no fewer than twenty times, and torn both knees badly enough to require half a dozen surgeries. He'd punctured his lung, lacerated his liver, and taken a hoof to the sack that swelled his nuts to the size of grapefruit.

"Can I learn that to fix myself up like that?" he asked.

"I wish," Nina said. "But no. Like I said, we're Unbound. No Carnal tricks for us."

"What if I joined them?"

"No can do. Technically, every psi mage has all seven energy strands, but we can tap one and only one. The others remain inert. So poor Brawley is stuck with only being able to rewrite the laws of physics."

"Hey, I'm not complaining. I just like to know what's possible. All right. So there's the Carnals and us. Who are the other five orders?"

"Well, you have mind mages or 'Benders.' They're telepaths and empaths."

She swerved to avoid hitting a chicken strutting across the street. "Then there are truth mages. We call them Seekers. Some of them can see the future."

Brawley nodded. He wasn't sure he'd want that ability, not unless he could change the things he saw.

Nina said, "Tech mages—we call them Gearheads—can

control machines. On the other side of the spectrum, you have the Beasties or beast mages."

"They control animals?" he guessed.

Her hair brushed his chin as she nodded. "Control them—or become them."

"That's different," he said. All of this was strange, but the idea of changing into an animal somehow seemed most far-fetched of all.

"It is different," she agreed. "I have a friend, Vixie, who lives in a Beastie compound out in the woods. She's a real fox. And I mean that in more than one way."

Nina turned down a quieter, more residential street. "But if you think that's weird, wait till you meet the arcane mages. We call them the Cosmics. See, psionics are like magic, right? But the energy we use comes from within, not without. Cosmics are different. They use their psionic power to draw on external energy sources, like mana, and to do crazy shit like open gates to other universes."

"That sounds like a bad idea," Brawley said.

"It is," Nina said. "And it's illegal now, thanks to the Order."

"The Order?"

"Yeah, they're kind of like our government, I guess, but maybe more like a police force. They take the best from each order, kind of like a psionic Delta Force, and solve big problems, like conflicts between orders or rogue psi mages."

Brawley nodded, taking it all in. He believed her, believed every word, but it was still hard to accept all this hocus-pocus bullshit. "How many people are psi mages?"

He felt her shoulders shrug against his chest. "Lots," she said. "More than you'd guess. A million in the US, maybe more."

Brawley whistled. "That's an awful lot. How come I've never heard of them?"

"I'm sure you've heard stories of weird things happening and people with strange abilities. Those stories are largely bullshit, but some are true—much to the chagrin of the Order. They make sure we keep a low profile. If the fuggles found out about us—"

"Fuggles?"

"Fucking Muggles," she laughed. "Normals. Norms. Normans and Normas. If they ever knew about us, they'd try to wipe us out. And that wouldn't be good for anybody. So the Order is really strict. No fucking with the fuggles. Ha— that sounds like a TV Show, doesn't it? 'Tonight on *Fucking with the Fuggles,* Gearhead prankster Fred hacks his fuggle boss's computer, and hilarity ensues.'"

Now it was Brawley's turn to laugh. What a surreal situation.

"But seriously," Nina said. "We're not supposed to use our powers around the fuggles. Let alone on them. If you do, they send someone like Remi after you."

"Not sure I'd mind her coming for me."

"Very funny, wiseass. Trust me, you don't want her on your trail."

Remi didn't strike him as a cop. "What is she, a bounty hunter?"

"I prefer to think of her as a professional pain in the ass, but yeah, she tracks people down for a living. Us and Fuggles. She has a bail bonds place on the other side of the island. And if I never see that place again, it'll be too soon."

"What did you do?"

"Tact, cowboy. You're not on the farm anymore. You don't just go asking impolite questions to a civilized lady like me."

He laughed. "You don't seem too delicate."

"I'm not," she said, "but if it's all the same to you, I'd rather not talk about Remi or our history."

Nina pulled into a narrow driveway between two stubby

bungalows half hidden in tropical foliage and parked along-side a wooden fence overgrown with flowering vines. They went through a gate into a tiny backyard dominated by a small swimming pool.

Moonlight rippled off the surface of the pool. Otherwise, it was surprisingly dark and private in the little backyard.

"Home sweet home," she said, and led him through a slider into the bungalow.

Nina flicked on the lights, revealing the tiny cottage's bright interior. The high-vaulted main room had a loveseat, a short shelf crammed with books, and a freestanding record player overtop a cubby packed with vinyl.

To the left, a small table and two chairs dominated a claustrophobic kitchenette. Further along the wall was a bathroom.

Against the far wall, a ladder led to a small, A-shaped loft. He could see the edge of a queen-sized mattress that fairly filled the sleeping nook.

Everything was bright and clean and surprisingly understated.

"Three hundred and fourteen square feet of heaven," Nina said. "Good things come in small packages. Want a beer?"

"Sure," he said, following her into the kitchen, where she handed him a Coors Light and grabbed a wine cooler for herself.

He thanked her, and they went back into the main room and sat on the loveseat. She folded her legs underneath her and let her leg flop against his thigh again.

"This is a nice place," Brawley said. "Not what I expected, but…"

Nina laughed. "And what did you expect? Some super secret psychic training lab?"

He took a pull off the beer. "I don't know what I expected, but it wasn't this. You don't look like someone who'd live here. I don't picture a girl with purple hair and combat boots living on page 39 of the Pottery Barn catalog."

"What?" Nina's mouth dropped wide open. She tried to look offended, but her smile ruined the effect. "Did you think I lived in a mosh pit?"

He shrugged. "Something like that."

"Don't judge a book by its cover. Or by its name... *Brawley*." She drew out his name, teasing him. "What if I heard your name and saw your cowboy boots and just assumed you lived on a ranch?"

"Then you would assume correctly, darlin," he said.

"Hmm," she said, and lifted her wine cooler to her grin. "So you're all predictable and boring, huh?"

"Boring's my middle name," Brawley said.

"Yeah right," she said. "So on this ranch of yours, do you ride horses and do cowboy shit?"

"I do."

"Do you throw lassos?"

"Yup."

"Do you... what's that phrase? Punch doggies?"

He laughed. "I do."

"What's that mean, anyway, punching doggies?"

"Tact, punk rocker. You don't just go asking a man about punching doggies."

Nina threw back her head and laughed. It was a pretty sound, wild and girlish and genuine. "I think maybe I like you, cowboy."

He held out his beer. "Well, I'll drink to that because I think maybe I like you, too, punk rocker."

They clinked their bottles. For a second, they just sat there, smiling, neither one of them saying a thing. Then Nina looked at his shirt and frowned.

Following her gaze, Brawley saw that blood had soaked through his white t-shirt, striping his chest in crimson.

"That's where the damned cat scratched me. You'd think she would've been grateful after I pulled her out of the ocean."

Nina's mismatched eyes lifted from his chest to his face, and a severely cute grin lit her face. "Never underestimate the dangers of a wet pussy."

Brawley laughed again. It felt good. He hadn't laughed this much since getting out of the hospital, that was for sure.

Nina finished her wine cooler, stood, and bent to place the empty on the little coffee table, giving Brawley a perfect view of her peach-shaped ass and toned hamstrings.

Then she straightened up, turned to face him, and gestured for Brawley to stand. He would've missed the view if she hadn't looked so delicious from the front, too.

He dragged his boots off the table, set his beer when they'd been propped, and stood looking down at this gorgeous girl, who was grinning playfully up at him.

He reached out to touch her, but his hand hit an invisible wall an inch from her shoulder.

"No shit," he said. "You're doing that?"

"I am," she said. "You cracked your power strand tonight," she said, "but you haven't opened it all the way yet. There's a lot to learn, and I'll be happy to teach you."

"I appreciate that."

"I'll teach you to recognize and draw the energy within you, how to shape it, how to reach out and grab the world by the balls."

As she said this, an invisible hand goosed his crotch.

"You know the best way to open your power strand wide open, cowboy? Find a nice telekinetic girl and fuck her cross-eyed, that's how."

5

B rawley reached for her again. This time, her invisible gate opened for him.

He flattened one hand against Nina's back and drew her toward him. The fingers of his other hand slid up the back of her neck and plunged into the purple locks.

Their mouths met, kissing softly at first then faster, harder, their tongues playing as their hands moved over each other, exploring.

Nina peeled the bloody t-shirt over his head, he untied her bikini top, and just like that, they had stripped to the waist.

Taking Nina by the shoulders, Brawley stepped back, held her at arm's length, and marveled at her naked perfection. Her perky breasts were large for her petite body but alluringly harmonious with her peach-perfect ass, which flared out lushly from her minuscule waist. "You are a beautiful woman," he said, meaning it.

"Thank you," she said, and he liked that she didn't blush or feel the need to make a joke or brush off the compliment altogether. He sensed no neediness in this woman, no insecurities or desperation or confusion, and that was very attractive to him. There is a difference between cockiness and confidence, and unless he was sorely mistaken, Nina fell on the right side of that line.

Nina paused to run her hands over his hard muscles, lingering here and there to trace some of his many scars.

It was a relief that she didn't ask about them.

They shucked the rest of their clothes.

It had been a long time for Brawley. Not that he was inexperienced.

He'd gotten with a couple of girls in high school. At eighteen, during his first season with the PBR tour, he'd sewn a lifetime of wild oats on his way to becoming Rookie of the Year. Jaded at nineteen, he'd started dodging the buckle bunnies. Well, mostly.

Since then, he'd had a few girlfriends, but none of those relationships had survived the long distances and insane demands of life on the road. Then he'd broken his neck, spent about a century in the hospital, and had been too busy sorting out his future to even consider getting frisky.

What made this moment even nicer was that Nina had no idea who he was.

When you're an eighteen-year-old kid from small town Texas, it's a rush to be recognized by anyone, let alone beautiful women. But that shit wears thin after a year or two of going town to town. He never stopped loving the fans and never ignored their requests for photos or signatures or a quick exchange, but there was a big difference between signing a program and having sex with a girl whose idea of foreplay was snapping a selfie with your gold buckle.

It got so you had a hard time trusting people's motivations.

Added to the appeal of his present anonymity was the alluring mystery of Nina herself. He knew almost nothing about the woman. He was attracted to her and enjoyed her company and wanted to know more about her and this strange power that they shared.

The moment crackled with energy.

Completely naked, Nina was breathtaking, head to toe.

Her mouth fell open, and for a few seconds, she just stared between his legs. "You really are a long, tall Texan," she said, reaching out to grip him by the root of his shaft. Her fingers didn't come close encircling his girth.

As Nina stroked him lightly, he kissed her collarbone and moved lower to suck her tiny, pink nipple into his mouth.

Nina purred with pleasure. Her free hand squeezed his balls.

Inhaling her heady floral aroma, he ran his hands down the curve of her back and filled them with her firm ass.

Nina's kisses came harder and more urgent, her breath quickening with desire.

His own desire was raging like a prairie fire now. Brawley wanted this woman. He reached between her legs and cupped her smooth and swollen mound, which was slick with excitement.

Nina trembled against him, her breath growing ragged as he caressed her silky folds.

Gripping his shaft in both hands, she said, "What do you say we skip the foreplay and open your power strand."

"Works for me," he said, still not really understanding the whole power strand thing. Grabbing Nina by the hips, he lifted her off the ground and positioned her overtop his erection. He paused there, looking into her lovely, mismatched eyes. "Ready?"

She threw her arms around his shoulders and wrapped her legs loosely around him. Her eyes were both nervous and excited. "Yeah, but go slow, okay? It's been a long time, and I've never been with anyone your size."

"We'll take it easy. You just let me know how you're doing."

Nina let out a shuddering breath and nodded like a rider ready to come out of the chute.

He lowered her inch by inch onto his hardness, pausing whenever she gasped or her eyes shot wide. She was warm and wet and wonderful, her tight channel gripping him as he lowered her bit by bit.

At last, she slid all the way down, tensing when he filled her. After a few seconds, she smiled and started squirming, lifting and lowering herself in short, pulsing motions.

"Yes," she breathed, her eyes fluttering shut.

When everything is right, there is nothing sweeter in the world than coupling with a new lover. They found their rhythm quickly and effortlessly, moving together like two halves of a single being.

This wasn't the sloppy pawing of two drunks slapping flesh during a hazy one-night stand.

Nor was this love-making, with its heavy emotional load and implications of commitment.

There was no power play, no history, no thought of the future beyond a mutual attraction and curiosity. Neither had chased the other. Nor had they drawn things out, giving the question of friendship time to shove its ugly face into the mix.

They were not friends. They did not love each other. But the powerful attraction between them was more than physical. And as they moved, Brawley felt a wave of bewildering affection for her.

It made no sense, this sudden stab of raw emotion. He liked this girl. A lot. More every second, it seemed. He liked her as if they had known one another for a long, sweet time. How was that possible?

Strange thoughts rose in his mind. He wanted to pleasure

Nina and keep her close, wanted to protect her and make her happy.

She smiled wide as her eyes locked on his and her body pumped rhythmically, sliding up and down his length. She moaned softly as she rode him. There was no bullshit with this woman, no fake-ass screaming or cutesy dirty talk.

"Oh," she said, and her eyes went wide. "Do you feel it?"

For a quarter of a second, he wondered what she meant by *it*—was she feeling this confusing surge of affection, too? —but then something clicked, and there was no longer any question about what she meant by *it*.

His dick was glowing. His dick, his balls, his whole pelvic region. That's how it felt. Like everything down there was glowing with warmth and vigor.

But this wonderful sensation wasn't contained to his flesh. It was swelling within her loins, too.

And somehow, he could feel that.

Before he could even try to make sense of what was happening, Nina whispered, "Faster now. That's it. Harder. Open me up, Brawley."

Squeezing her firm ass, he pumped faster and harder. Their flesh smacked together in perfect rhythm, beat for beat, pounding away, while this other thing, this channel of energy coursing through them, spread euphorically away from their coupled sexes, filling their limbs and torsos with sizzling warmth.

He barked laughter, surprised by a rush of elation and power.

Nina beamed, writhing with pleasure.

As this supernatural energy bound them, Brawley's feelings of affection and protectiveness for Nina grew. There was no weakness in this burgeoning adoration. Quite the opposite, in fact. With ever thrust, his feelings for her grew, and with every increase, he felt stronger, more dominant, more territorial.

"Yes," she cried. "Keep going, babe. That's it. Tap that strand. Almost there now. So amazing. Come on, Brawley. Tap it. Let me feel your power."

Brawley growled, thrusting away as the suffusing energy rose through their bodies.

Nina's breaths came faster and faster.

Then the energy rushed into their heads. An unbroken u-shaped flow of power formed between them, running from her brain through their bodies into his own mind.

Nina thrust into him—not with her body, which tensed now with impending climax—but with her mind, her psionic power. A wave of bright red energy rushed out of her body and through his dick, raced up his body like magma shooting up an erupting volcano, and burst in an vermillion explosion within his skull, where he felt something crack wide open.

Brawley roared, and his mind bucked like it was strapped to the rankest bull in the world. A fountain of power burst from the crown of his skull, arched into the air, and punched straight down through Nina's purple tresses. A river of psionic force rushed out of his mind, flashed through her quivering body, and slammed back into him, where it joined the energy still gushing from his newly opened strand.

For several seconds, they both cried out in garbled streams of euphoria like enraptured worshipers prophesying in tongues.

Her body rode his, and they both rode a ring of pulsing psionic power.

They gasped in unison, locked in a mutual paralysis of awe and pleasure—then cried out at the same instant, their bodies bucking wildly as they exploded in simultaneous orgasm.

Brawley was aware of Nina clinging to him, shuddering

and screaming and soaking him with her juices as his entire body convulsed with waves of ecstasy and he pumped her full of hot seed.

When the epic waves of their shared climax finally ebbed away, the ring of power split apart at its apex, parted at their lower point of pulsing union, and unbundled, a portion of the energy receding back into each individual.

Power whipped up Brawley's core and flooded his skull. A second later, the ruby inferno imploded, crushing into a bright singularity at the center of his mind before winking out altogether.

"What the fuck?" Nina heaved, going limp in his arms. "What the fuck?" Her panting voice sounded amazed, almost stunned—which made perfect sense to Brawley, because that's exactly how he felt in that moment.

He lowered her onto the loveseat, kissing her softly as Nina said over and over in an incredulous mumble, "What the fuck? What the fuck?"

————

AS THE WORDS TUMBLED FROM HER MOUTH IN SHOCKED murmurs, they echoed loudly within Nina's mind.

What the fuck? What the fuck?

Over the course of her twenty-two years, Nina had been with three other men. Well, a boy and two boyish men, if she was honest. Her fuggle boyfriend in high school and two other guys since, both of whom were Unbound, and both of whose strands she had opened, having heard that could be fun and beneficial.

Opening those strands had been a kick, and she had felt the little surge of power people talked about.

But this…

This was un-fucking-believable.

Brawley was big and strong. Handsome and fun. Refreshingly different. And a man. In fact, after meeting him, despite the short time they had been together, she suspected he might be the first real man she'd ever met.

And yet what she had felt, what she was *still* feeling for fuck's sake, had nothing to do with his big hands, bright smile, or the courage and integrity she could feel coming off him in waves.

It was his strand.

She knew she had more juice than most psi mages. Much more, in fact. Sage, who as a Seeker felt the need to quantify such matters in numerical ratings, claimed Nina's psi score was 140. Basically, where other psi mages drew on the psionic equivalent of AA batteries or maybe a C cell, Nina's mind hooked into a frigging car battery.

And Brawley? This cowboy was packing a nuclear power plant.

The rush of energy had formed some kind of crazy power ring. She'd never even heard of anything like that. For a moment, she wasn't even in herself anymore. Not properly, anyway. Skewered on the ring with him, she had lost her sense of self, as if they had blurred into each other. The rush transported Nina out of herself into a transcendent bliss of union with Brawley, where everything was power and pleasure.

And then the orgasm.

Again, what the fuck?

Never in all her life had she so much as fantasized that anything could feel that good. All of her had climaxed. Not just her body but her mind, her energy, her fucking soul… and Brawley, too. All of him. She had felt it. His pleasure as well as hers… because in that moment, they were the same thing. They had literally climaxed together, their minds and bodies, energies and souls intermingled.

Everything had changed.

She felt shaken yet elated. And supercharged with psionic energy. Every psi mage enjoyed coupling with a psychic virgin because it was fun to usher them into the psionic community and because you got a boost from opening their strand. Not a ton but a noticeable little pick-me-up. Like your psionic storehouse knocked back a cup of coffee, the slight caffeine lift of which would never fade.

But this...

What the fuck?

Her trusty car battery felt more akin to a jet engine now. Psionic energy thrummed at the center of her mind, ready for action. She felt like she could generate enough force to blast a bank vault open or tear an armored car in half.

Not that she would do those things. And that's when she realized that regardless of what had just happened to her, she needed to hide this new power from her father. Otherwise, he would force her back into the life she had never wanted in the first place.

But then she realized the error in her thinking, and inwardly, she smiled.

No, he wouldn't force her. He would *try* to force her.

Good luck with that now, Dad.

Brawley had given her so much.

Not just the best orgasm of her life but also enough power that she would never have to take her dad's shit again. Hell, if she was even half as powerful as she felt right now, she wouldn't be taking anyone's shit ever again.

Not that Brawley would ever let somebody give me shit, she thought warmly. Then she stifled a laugh, because she had never before entertained a thought like that about any man.

Nina knew she was a complicated girl. A hot mess, honestly. A study in wasted potential. A twenty-two-year-old ex-con standing at a crossroads, trapped between a world she'd sworn off and a world she couldn't seem to understand, much less join. And whenever the square, work-a-day world rolled its eyes at her, surly pride and the promise of a quick buck whispered from the shadows of her past.

And that whisper was always the same voice. Her father's.

Nina was a confident woman, but for a long time, she had been drifting, coasting along, skimming across the surface of total disaster. She could still smile, still laugh, still enjoy simple things, but she had lost her faith in people... and in no person more than in herself.

Despite her quick smiles and easy laughter, she had formed a hard shell against the world. She got along with nearly everyone but kept all of them at arm's length.

All of them but her kid brother, David, that was. But his mother made it almost impossible for Nina to see him.

Which had, in its way, strengthened Nina's armor against the world.

Brawley, however, had smashed through her shell, not just busting a hole in her defenses but vaporizing them. And suddenly, Nina Mack, the supposedly jaded, streetwise, independent woman, was crushing as hard as a giggly schoolgirl.

This man with his scars and his drawl and ridiculous name—*Brawley,* for crying out loud; who names their son *Brawley?*—had swept her completely off her feet.

It bewildered Nina to admit to herself, but she was smitten.

She wanted to fawn for him. Wanted to cavort. Wanted to spread herself at his feet in naked submission, bowing low and crossing her wrists like the girls in those Gor books she'd read during high school.

And that, friends, made no damn sense at all.

She was a strong, autonomous woman. Always had been. Only one man had ever been able to manipulate or intimidate her, and that was her father, a powerful telepath who knew her every switch in her psychological fuse box and never hesitated to throw any or all of them to get what he wanted.

Getting locked up had strengthened Nina against even him. No thanks to the lame ass counselors, though. Jail just sucked. Hard. Every minute of every day. The unrelenting lack of freedom; the way some of the guards were such petty assholes; the starchy, ugly uniform; the shitty food and the way it played hell on your complexion; the sour smell of the place, all those bodies crammed together, hating; and most of all the other inmates.

These women sat around, talking shit and telling lies, swinging back and forth between swearing fierce allegiance to their kids and barking about how they were stone-cold bad asses. Night and day, these bitches flapped their lips, trying so hard to sell their bullshit that they started buying it themselves. Hell, they talked so much they couldn't even recognize how frequently they contradicted themselves.

It was maddening.

Jail punched Nina hard enough that she had since found the strength to resist her father's manipulations. She had stuck to the straight and narrow, and even though she had not yet found a place in the fuggles' work-a-day world, she would not deviate from her course, because nothing mattered to her more than staying the fuck out of jail.

But if her Dad found out about her new power, he would try anything and everything to rope her into another job.

One last score, he would croon. The very last. A safe bet. And they would be set forever.

She wanted no more of his bullshit.

All she seemed to want in this moment of afterglow was more Brawley. And not just more sex. Their melding had done something to her. Something confounding and, frankly, absurd.

She could imagine nothing more appealing than bowing down to Brawley and pledging herself to him, mind, body, and soul, in total and eternal submission.

Which was fucking crazy, thank you very much.

She could feel some kind of mysterious psychic webbing lingering faintly between them, as if fibers of their psionic essences had woven invisibly together.

She wanted to play with him. Protect him. Pamper him.

Forever.

I'm drunk, she thought. *Drunk on psi power. Brawley overloaded me somehow. But this will pass. I'll return to myself and laugh about the whole thing.*

Right now, though?

Right now, her eyes were riveted to that big, thick pole of his. And judging by its size and extreme rigidity, Brawley was feeling pretty good about her, too.

She reached out and took him in her hand.

What's the harm in having a little more fun? she thought, opening her mouth and struggling to stretch her lips over the swollen head of his massive cock. *If nothing else, it'll take my mind off these crazy emotions.*

———

HOURS LATER, AS THE PALE LIGHT OF EARLY DAWN BROKE faintly through the windows, they came together for what seemed to Brawley the millionth time. For the last couple of hours, they had been trying to sleep, cuddled together in Nina's loft mattress. But then one of them would shift his or her weight or brush up against the other, and they'd be at it again.

To hell with it. Both of them were too wired and too happy to sleep. All they wanted to do was talk and fuck and cuddle.

Nina kissed him deeply and flopped back with a sigh. Her body glistened with perspiration, and her hair had collapsed into a lavender tangle.

Brawley stood. Or stooped, anyway. There wasn't enough clearance in the loft for him to straighten all the way.

Parting with Nina's flesh, losing the touch of her skin against his, was almost painful. He considered that for a moment.

It had something to do with the crazy ring of psionic power that had skewered them the first time they'd done it. Though that force had whipped away deep into their minds, ethereal tendrils of mystic energy still bound them.

Nina stared up at him with a knowing smile.

He gazed down into her mismatched eyes and felt a fresh surge of overwhelming affection. With it came a wave of protectiveness so fierce that territorial hackles rose along his consciousness.

He had never been a possessive or jealous man. But in this moment, he understood one thing above all others.

Nina was his woman now.

His and his alone. He would protect and care for her and make her life better. And if anyone tried to harm her…

Where were these crazy-ass thoughts coming from?

"All right," he said, pulling up his jeans. "Breakfast. I mean it this time. No more of your tricks."

Nina sat up, grinning slyly. She stretched, arching her back, and twisted at the waist, making her sweaty breasts wobble irresistibly. "What do you mean, tricks?"

"You know what I mean, you little temptress," he said, buckling his belt. Damned if he wasn't getting hard again. "Now come on. I need bacon like a spider needs a fly."

"That's a big buckle," Nina said, unhooking his belt. "Where do you even buy one that size?"

Brawley laughed, staring not at the buckle but at her

unbelievable breasts, which pressed hypnotically together, wiggling between her arms as she worked with his belt.

"You can't buy that buckle," he said. "You gotta earn it."

Tilting the buckle, she read, "World champion? Wait… is this real?"

He nodded.

Studying the buckle, she said, "So you're a world champion what… bull rider?"

He nodded again.

She filled the room with her beautiful, unbridled laughter. "That's crazy. I mean, I don't know whether that's the coolest thing I've ever heard or the corniest."

"It's the coolest," he said with a grin. "Now put on some damned clothes, or I'm going to bend you over and do you again."

She smirked. "Big talker. You have another round in you, champ?"

He gestured toward the erection jutting from his waistband. "What's it look like to you?"

"Looks like I hit the jackpot." She rolled onto her stomach, lifted her perfect ass into the air, and grinned over one shoulder. "You going to ride me like a bull this time?"

He shucked his jeans and jockeys and gave her ass a light smack. "I'll hold on for eight seconds."

She twitched her ass back and forth. "You'd better hold on for a lot longer than that, cowboy."

Lining himself up with her swollen sex, he said, "Be careful what you wish for, darlin'," and plunged deep inside her.

———

LATER, BRAWLEY PULLED ON HIS JOCKEY SHORTS AND STARTED hunting his socks.

Nina, watching with an amused expression, said, "I can't believe I just slept with a man who wears tighty whiteys."

"I don't recall much sleeping."

"You know what I mean. And tall white socks?"

"White socks is all I wear. Same goes for jockey shorts. We gonna eat or what?"

She rose and crossed the loft to a small dresser, rifled through the drawers, and came back with shorts, a t-shirt, and fishnet stockings, which he paused to watch her pull over her shapely legs.

"Truth be told," she said, fastening one of the garters, "your power doesn't make sense. It's too much. Honestly, I can't even begin to wrap my head around it. I mean, I thought you'd give me a little boost, but... *wow*. What are you doing later?"

"Hell, I don't know. Eating breakfast. After that, I'm open. What do got in mind?"

"More of this," she said, gesturing toward the bed and the tangled sheets soaked in their juices.

"That's a plan I can get behind."

"And on top of, I hope," Nina said with another sly grin. "Then I'm taking you to meet my Seeker friend, Sage. If anybody can figure out how it's possible for you to be packing all that power in your mind, it's her. I can't wait to hear your psi score and what she says about your aura."

6

Other than a couple of hours of shocking unconsciousness back at Eden House, Brawley hadn't slept a wink, but he felt great. Energized, optimistic, relaxed. And unbelievably horny, despite a night of ceaseless and torrid sex. Part of this was the psionic boost, of course. But part of it was Nina.

She looked hot sitting there across the small metal table of the cafe, sipping black coffee from the big, white, ceramic mug and reading the local paper with one leg crossed over the other, rocking her fingerless gloves, fishnet stockings, and combat boots for all the world to see.

Yonder sits my heart, he thought, surprising himself with the notion. But it was true. Rather than receding over the hours, the powerful affection and possessiveness he felt toward Nina had only continued to grow stronger.

The morning was warm and sunny with a pleasant breeze, perfect for eating outside. The restaurant was packed, and several couples stood in line by the hostess's podium.

Brawley liked that some of the people had dogs with

them. He also liked that the place, much like Blue Heaven, had a sizeable population of resident cats and chickens.

At the curb near his boot, a mourning dove pecked a shred of croissant. There was very little vehicular traffic. People strolled past or rolled by on old-school bicycles painted in pastel shades. In the distance, a rooster crowed.

"This is a nice town," he said.

Nina nodded, sipping her coffee. "It is. So when are you moving here?"

He smiled but shook his head. "Not me, darlin. I wouldn't mind spending a week or two here now and then. Hell, maybe even a month or two in the winter. But I'll never leave God's country."

"What's so great about Texas?"

"It's Texas."

"Very funny, cowboy. Could you humor me and be a little more specific?"

"Brisket, for starters. Family. The ranch. Hell, everything. Life's different there. Slower. You got enough space to stretch your legs and catch your breath. People are laid back. Hospitable, too."

"Hospitable?" She arched a dubious eyebrow. "You were my guest last night. You don't call that hospitable?"

He laughed. "Good point. I'd have to say you're the most hospitable person I've ever met. You'll fit right in when you move to Texas."

Nina laughed. "Not me, cowboy."

"So you say now." His feelings toward her were bold and energized, confident and dominant, yet tender. He did the emotional math and surprised himself.

"What are you grinning at?" she asked.

"I just realized something. I love you."

Nina beamed, then tried to cover it by rolling her eyes. "You don't even know my last name."

"That doesn't matter. What is it, anyway?"

"What's yours?"

"Hayes."

"Brawley Hayes?"

"Brawley Peckinpah Hayes, if you please."

She laughed but it was faint and distracted. "What kind of a name is Peckinpah?"

"My grandma was a big fan of The Wild Bunch."

"You lost me. Is that a movie?"

Brawley stared at her for a second without speaking. "What's yours?"

"Mack."

"Nina Mack."

She nodded. "Nina Anastasia Mack... if you please."

"Well then, Nina Anastasia Mack, I reckon I love you."

Again, she rolled her eyes. And again, it was less than convincing. "Go lay down and rest a while, and you'll come to your senses."

"No I won't, not if you mean I'll change my mind. I love you, plain and simple. And you love me."

Her laughter was incredulous. "Now you're really talking crazy."

"No I'm not, and you know it. But I won't badger you."

"Good," she said, and made a show of picking up the newspaper. "Drink your coffee and the feeling will pass."

"No, it won't. Not ever."

"Oh shit," Nina said with a smile. "I knew you were too good to be true. You're one of those creepy stalker types, aren't you?"

"You'd be heartbroken if I wasn't."

"Yeah right."

"Don't you worry, darlin. That's a line you'll never have to toe. I won't break your heart, and I sure as hell won't walk out on you. Ever."

Nina stared into his eyes and smiled. Really smiled. It was a small smile, tight with sudden hope.

But then a cloud of some conflicting emotion drifted over her features. Her eyes lost focus for a second, staring out into the reaches of some painful memory, and the smile faded.

And Brawley understood that she had been hurt in the past. Deeply.

"Yeah," she said. "Well don't go making promises you can't keep."

"I keep my promises," Brawley said. "Always."

They were silent for a time, Nina reading the paper, Brawley watching the world go by and wondering if anyone could hear his stomach growl every time a server walked past with a tray of steaming food.

Nina turned the paper in his direction. "Look. You're famous."

"Huh?"

She had it open to the police log. She pointed to a specific section and shoved the paper into his hands with a smirk.

Motorcyclist Leads Police on High-speed Chase.

Brawley glanced up from the headline. "I'm missing the joke, darlin."

"There is no joke," she said. "Look again, noob. Harder."

He humored her, looked again, and still saw three paragraphs about some jackass flying down Route 1 on a Kawasaki.

"Concentrate," Nina said. "You're looking *at* the article. Look *through* it."

He stared for a second longer. Then, just as he was about to hand back the paper and call her crazy, the ink wavered. All at once, it was too blurry to read. A second later, the letters cleared again… in a completely different arrangement.

Psi Display Disturbs Mallory Square Sunset Celebration.

"What the hell?"

Officials are investigating reports of psionic activity at last night's sunset celebration. According to social media posts by dozens of Normal eyewitnesses, a cat owned by Charles "The Cat Wizard" McDonough, a registered Bestial originally from Philadelphia, Pennsylvania, flew suddenly into the ocean by means of what appeared to be supernatural levitation.

An unknown man, described by the Normals as a tall, white male in his mid-twenties, allegedly intervened and rescued the cat by telekinetic means, lifting the animal from the water and drawing it one hundred feet to safety. Dozens of Normals reported the supernatural occurrence via social media, where the claims appear to be generating what local authorities are deeming "potentially unfortunate" interest. McDonough was not available for questioning.

If you have any information concerning Mr. McDonough or the incident, please contact your local Order authorities.

"What is this?" he asked, dumbfounded.

Nina leaned forward, whispering. "Psi writing. Our news beneath theirs. You'll see psi script on papers, magazines, and signs in every decent-sized town in America."

He flipped through the pages, pausing to let each page beneath the page come clear. He saw global, national, state, and local headlines. Editorials, ads, classifieds, all the things you would expect from a newspaper.

It was mind-boggling. And yet... shockingly, even disappointingly, normal.

"Female telepath, 36, ISO male telepath, 25-35," he read aloud.

Nina shrugged. "Dating can be a bitch for psi mages. Especially for telepaths."

He turned his attention to the advertisements.

Psi Pet Trainers.

Psi-D Identity Protection.

Elemental Excavation.

"It's all so… real," he said. "So normal."

"*Normal* is a loaded word in our community," Nina said. "Better to say it's all so mundane. But yeah, at the end of the day, we're still just people, I'm afraid. We can do some incredible shit, but our lives still revolve around weddings and funerals like everybody else."

Turning back to the crime log, he said, "Is this going to be a problem?"

"We'll see. If you turned yourself in and explained what happened, the Order would probably just read you the riot act, register you, and offer support via the local Unbound post over on Flagler."

Reading her voice, he said, "But…"

"But the less those fuckers know about you, the better. When you register, you don't want an asterisk by your name."

He nodded. "What if I don't want to register at all?"

"Bold move. It's one thing, being a clueless orphan sucker punched by the whole thing. It's quite another to reject the community altogether."

Brawley leaned back and crossed his arms over his chest. "I don't want people in my business."

"You don't want to register, don't register." She sipped her coffee. "But don't get caught up in anything, or they'll hang you out to dry."

"I have a bad habit of getting caught up in stuff. This guy Junior and his buddies, how come they aren't in trouble? They weren't exactly subtle, throwing the cat in the ocean like that."

"Audacity beats alibi. One shocking, abrupt event." She snapped her fingers. "Then the cat's in the water, and that's what people are worried about. No one suspected them, and even if the story hit social media—and that's what the Order really cares about—it's too short and weird to gain traction.

A cat flies in the water. There's no narrative. But if you add some heroic Texan to the mix, have him waving his arms like a madman, and then have the cat float from the water straight to him…"

Brawley nodded. "So I drew attention to the psi mafia."

"Like a champ," she said. "If they were on official orders, you just pissed off an international organization that hates making the headlines."

"And if they weren't on official orders?"

"Side jobs are a big no-no in the psi mob. Those three would do anything to keep from getting in trouble with their boss. And since we're talking about Junior Dutchman, that boss also happens to be his father, so double-whammy. Meanwhile, I don't know whether the Bestial is 'unavailable for questioning' because he's skipped town or because the psi mob whacked him. The only thing I really know for sure is that those assholes saw me with you."

"Oh shit," he said, and something dark and fierce rose within him. "If they try to—"

"Pie?" a cheery voice asked behind him.

Nina lit up like a six-year-old on Christmas morning. "Right here."

The waitress set a slice of key lime pie in front of Nina. Balancing her tray on the edge of the small table, she turned to Brawley. "Well, somebody's hungry this morning."

"Yes, ma'am."

Setting the plates before him, she said, "Western omelet with extra jalapenos. A double order of bacon. Home fries with sausage gravy. White toast with butter. Jam and ketchup are on the table. Can I get you folks anything else?"

"More coffee for me, please," Nina said, and shoved a forkful of pie into her mouth. Her eyes fluttered shut in apparent ecstasy.

"Y'all have any hot sauce?" Brawley asked.

"Tabasco all right?"

Brawley wasn't a big fan of Tabasco. He liked taste or heat. Often times, you had to surrender one for the other. Tabasco dwelled in a weird twilight zone that didn't deliver much of either.

But it was better than no hot sauce at all. "That'd be great. Thank you, ma'am."

After the waitress left, Brawley said, "If those assholes—"

"Please don't," Nina said. "I'll be fine, and if you insist, we can talk about them later. Right now, I just want to enjoy my pie." She took another bite and sat there with her eyes shut, grinning like a little girl dreaming of unicorns and lollipops.

They set to eating. The food was amazing, and Brawley was hungry. Typically, he ate like a dog. Once or twice a day, ravenously, as much as you put before him.

Nina watched him, looking amused. "All that bacon and gravy can't be good for you."

He chuckled, sopping up gravy with his toast. "I don't take health tips from girls who only eat pie for breakfast."

She gave him a smart-ass grin. "Not just pie. Pie and coffee."

When they finished, Brawley leaned back, feeling good.

"All right," Nina said. "Now that you've eaten, it's time to train."

"Train?"

"First things first. You need to learn to locate your power."

"What, here?"

"Sure. Why not?"

He gestured to the busy café porch. "Wouldn't your place be better?"

"Sure, if we were a pair of hermits. But we don't live our lives shut away from the world. You might as well get used to locating your energy with distractions."

He nodded. It made sense, when she put it that way.

"Just don't go acting like some kind of nut again, like you did at Mallory Square, okay?" She mimicked him, bugging out her pretty eyes and waving her arms crazily.

"Blow me," he said.

"Gladly," Nina said. "But first you have to practice."

She explained how to locate his power. First, he needed to still his mind. Then he had to wait. Eventually, he would feel a light tickle in his mind.

"Then what?" he asked.

"One step at a time, cowboy," she said. "I'll be shocked if you can find it today or even this week. It usually takes a while. Weeks, usually. Months, sometimes. But you have to start somewhere."

"If it's so hard to do, how come I was able to save the cat?"

"Because you needed to. It was a primal moment, do or die. That happens a lot with first timers. Some primal emotion—anger, desperation, fear—will pop their cherry. Next thing you know, a ninety-eight-pound weakling is lifting a car off her kid brother."

"All right. Let me take a shot at this." He shut his eyes and tried to clear his mind.

"You don't have to shut your eyes," Nina said.

"Hush, woman. I'm trying to concentrate."

"You look like you have to fart," she laughed.

"There it is," he said.

"What, the tickle?"

He nodded.

"Bullshit," she said.

"But it's not really a tickle," he said, considering the weird sensation in his mind. "It's stronger than a tickle. And warm. Like a burning flame, only without the light."

"Holy shit," Nina said. "You're serious. See if you can draw it."

He popped one eye open. "The hell does that mean, draw it?"

Nina looked excited. "Once you find your power, you have to draw it together. You can't force it, though. You have to coax the energy. It wants to work with you. Hell, it *is* you. But right now the power is still deep down inside, buried alongside the inert strands that the other orders use."

Brawley concentrated, feeling stupid. He had no idea what he was supposed to be doing. "Any tips on how to coax it? I feel about like a one-legged cat trying to bury a turd on a frozen lake."

"Just focus on the invisible flame," she said. "Think happy thoughts. Imagine it coming toward you."

"Toward me? It's already inside me."

"Toward your consciousness, your will."

For a moment, he focused on the sensation, which grew more powerful. After a while, he had a clearer sense of his will as an entity unto itself, one part of a larger organism. His mind, he supposed. Like all these years, his consciousness had been floating obliviously in the middle of an enormous, pitch-black cave.

He mentally beckoned the energy toward his will, but the flame merely flickered. He imagined the strand responding to him, stretching out toward his consciousness, but it still didn't budge.

So he switched tacks.

Rather than drawing the strand toward him, he willed his consciousness forward in the void, moving closer to the power, which grew stronger as he approached. He imagined reaching out, imagined seizing hold of the power but realized the power wasn't a single rope that he could latch onto. He had a sense of multiple lines of power wavering like kelp.

One strand was far more distinct than the others. He focused on this wavering thing, and a section of his will unparcelled itself from his consciousness and reached out like a hand to grasp the strand.

Yes.

Gripping the strand, he felt warmth and mass and a constant buzzing, as if he had seized an overloaded power cable. He tried to haul back on the strand, tried to draw it toward him the way Nina described, but the buzzing cord slipped away like a greased eel.

Several times, he tried and failed.

"More coffee?" the waitress asked.

"None for me, thanks," Nina said.

"No thank you, ma'am," Brawley said with a quick smile. He was impatient, wanting to rush back inside his skull. "Just the check, please."

The waitress left, and Nina laid a hand on Brawley's. "Take a break, babe. Tell me what's happening in there."

He explained what he'd been doing and how frustrated he was not to be able to draw the power. Taking the time to explain this only fueled his frustration. All he really wanted to do was go back in and try again.

Brawley believed in the power of repetition. More than believed in it. It was part of him and had been ever since he was a kid and his dad had brought home an oil drum and rigged up a bucking barrel.

Brawley rode that drum hours every day. While other kids were running off to fish or play ball, he'd sit on his barrel, rolling back and forth with one arm in the air, finding his rhythm and developing his balance.

Then he'd gotten the medicine ball. Since then, if somebody stopped to visit, they'd likely find Brawley standing on the ball. He'd stand there eating a bowl of Fruit Loops and talk to whoever had stopped.

So yeah, it was in his nature to practice a thing, and he was ready to dive back in.

But Nina was blown away. "I can't believe you were able to do all that," she said again. "I mean, I've never heard of such a thing. You moved your will toward the strand?"

He nodded. "Well, the strands. There was a bunch of them."

Her mouth fell open. "We have to go see Sage."

"Hold on now. I want to have another go at this."

"Later," she said. "Please? You have your whole life to practice. I can't wait to see the look on Sage's face. You have serious power. She's gonna flip when she sees your aura. But let's get going. I have to work later."

"What do you do?"

She frowned. "I deliver for a Chinese restaurant."

"Call in sick."

She shook her head. "My boss is an asshole. He'll fire me if I call out."

"Quit then," Brawley said, hating the idea of some asshole lording power over Nina.

"Quit, huh? And how am I supposed to pay the rent?"

"You don't have to work. I got plenty of money for both of us."

As if on cue, the waitress showed up with their check. Brawley took it and pulled out his billfold.

"I'll pay for my pie," Nina said.

"Forget it," he said, laying out the bills.

"So you're proposing what, exactly," she asked. "That I become a kept woman?"

"Call it what you want. I'm just saying you don't have to worry about money."

"Bullshit," she said, throwing bills onto the pile. "I pay my own way."

"I respect that," he said. "But if you get sick of working, quit, and I'll take care of things."

She shook her head. "I wouldn't want to owe you."

"You wouldn't owe me shit. I'm not lending you money. I'm giving it to you. No strings attached. It's just money."

"Just money," she snorted. She looked briefly troubled. Then she sipped her coffee and said, "Please tell me you're not a drug dealer or something. I really can't afford to be dating criminals."

He laughed. "Not hardly."

"Okay, good. So where did you come into all this moola, Mr. Moneybags? Something to do with that?" She pointed at his big gold buckle.

Brawley nodded. "I won two million dollars riding bulls."

She choked on her coffee. "Get the fuck out of here."

"Two-and-a-half, if you count endorsements. I had offers for a while, but my agent held out until I won the title last year, figuring I'd get bigger deals. Trouble is, after I won the title last year, I only got the signing bonus and two royalty payments before I broke my neck. And that was all she wrote. No more bull riding, no more endorsements."

Nina put her hand on his. "I'm sorry, Brawley. Do you miss it?"

He laughed bitterly. "I do. Don't ask me why I'd miss running all over the country and getting stomped, but I really do."

They sat quietly for a while, sipping their coffee.

Then Brawley said, "The way they pay out the championship, you get ten percent per year, minus taxes and agent's commission. Then you got your insurance payments. This year, I threw most of my dough in the bank. But last year, I blew through the money. Helped my parents out a little, bought an RV."

She grinned like he'd cracked a joke. "An RV? One of those big camper things?"

"That's right. You are sitting across from a bona fide Winnebago warrior."

She laughed. "You certainly are a character."

"So says the girl with purple hair."

"Pfft. What kind of lunatic drives a camper around?"

"A six-foot-two lunatic tired of cramming into a truck with three or four other cowboys and smelling farts for a thousand miles at a stretch. Besides, you take one look at my RV, you'll stop talking all that shit."

Her smile got bigger. "Wait, it's not back in Texas? You drove it here?"

"It's parked across the island by the grocery store. You treat me right, I'll give you the grand tour later."

"The grand tour of your RV, huh? Brawley Hayes, are you trying to seduce me?"

"You know it, girl."

She laughed. "Well, in that case, I accept. But later. I'm dying to hear what Sage has to say about your aura."

"All right. But first I have to swing by my hotel. Checkout's at eleven. You going to invite me to crash at your place or what?"

7

As they were crossing town, a rough-looking homeless woman pushing a shopping cart stopped and stared at Brawley, mumbling gibberish.

"I think she liked you," Nina joked after they'd turned the corner.

Brawley told her about the crazy bastard with the bugs in his beard.

"Fucking Chaotics," she said. "We get a lot of them here. Key West is a magnet for psi mages who've lost their way."

Brawley nodded. Her comment hit a little close to home. It was his dreams that had dragged him here, after all, not a travel brochure. "What, exactly, do you mean by Chaotics?"

"I told you about the seven orders," she said. "We're the Unbound. Sage is a Seeker. Remi's a Carnal. That Cat Wizard guy was a Bestial. You saw ads for Gearheads and Benders. I mentioned the weird-ass Cosmics and *the* Order. Finally, you have people who break ties with their Orders and go off on their own. We call them Chaotics.

"A lot of them are homeless. They live on the streets, in tent cities, or in hobo jungles. Then you have your fugue-state types. They snap, lose their shit, and leave it all behind. They move halfway across the country, grow a beard, and spend the rest of their lives answering to "Fred" or "Joe" and washing dishes in the land of cash and shadows, waiting to die.

"Sadly, most of the Chaotics are crazy. Tons of mental health issues in our community, especially among Benders and Cosmics. Seekers, too."

They turned down another street. This part of Key West was quiet and residential.

"But not all Chaotics are crazy," Nina said. "You see exiles, gangs, fugitives. Communes in the woods, cults, anti-establishment compounds. And there's the Psychic Underground living in the tunnels beneath Manhattan. To me, you'd have to be both homeless and crazy to live down there like moles, but word on the street is they're organized. Some people say Clarissa Lemay is down there, calling the shots."

"Who's she?"

Nina laughed. "It's crazy how much there is to tell you. Every psi kid on the planet is scared shitless of Clarissa Lemay. She's the bogeywoman, the last power mage on Earth if you believe the stories, but personally, I think it's a bunch of—"

"Nina Mack," a deep voice said. A man in a blue and silver track suit stepped from the driver's seat of a black Escalade and blocked their way.

Blocking the sidewalk was easier for this guy than it would be for most people. He was a big bastard. Thick bones, lots of muscle, and a big gut, too, like a former NFL linebacker gone to seed. The guy was Brawley's height but probably three hundred pounds, maybe more.

He had a flat face. Dozens of scars twisted like pale rivers across the forest of black stubble atop his shaved head. A pair of tattooed teardrops dripped from the corner of one eye.

Beneath the unzipped windbreaker, he wore a black V-neck t-shirt, which contrasted sharply with the half dozen bright yellow chains gleaming on his neck and the many rings spread across his fat fingers like a pair of gold-plated brass knuckles.

"Gordo," Nina chimed. "What a pleasant surprise."

Gordo nodded toward the SUV. "Get in. Mr. Dutchman wants to see you."

"Hmm," Nina said. "Would that be Mr. Dutchman, Senior or Junior?"

"Junior. Now get in." Gordo barely glanced at Brawley. Most people—and especially burly guys—took one look at Brawley and dismissed him as skinny. They'd seen too many movies and thought a man had to beef up like a steer to be strong. "And who the fuck are you supposed to be, her boyfriend?"

"I'm her man friend," Brawley said.

Gordo made a whisking motion with his stubby, ring-studded fingers. "You go bye-bye and have a nice day."

"You know, I'd really love to come with you," Nina said, edging sideways, "but we're running late. Tell Junior I said hey and I'll be looking for him. 'Kay? Bye-ee!"

She twiddled her fingers at the hulking hard ass and tried to scoot past him.

"You're coming with me," Gordo said, and he grabbed Nina by the wrist.

Brawley nailed him.

Gordo must have written him off, because he never saw the punch coming. The hellacious right cross caught him square on the hinge of the jaw.

Brawley followed up with a looping left hook that smashed Gordo straight in the nose.

Brawley knew he had dynamite in both hands, but this big fucker didn't even buckle. That thick neck and lumpy head of his had taken the shots, no problem. Gordo just hunched into the blows and started turning toward Brawley, his flat nose streaming blood.

But rather than taking a swing or going for a tackle, Gordo reached around toward the small of his back.

Which meant he was packing. And which furthermore gave Brawley time to hit him again—and the motivation to take the big bastard out any way he could.

So Brawley said to hell with the punches and drove a stomping kick down on the big man's leg just above the knee.

This time, Gordo buckled. But he stayed on his feet and kept going for his piece, so Brawley stomped him again.

Gordo's leg gave with a loud cracking sound. The big man cried out and fell face-first onto the sidewalk.

Brawley leaned over, jerked up Gordo's windbreaker, and pulled a stubby automatic from the screaming man's waistband.

Jamming a knee into Gordo's spine, he seized the back of his muscular neck and pressed the muzzle against the stubbly temple. "Stop your screaming and listen," Brawley said. "This? What happened to you? It's nothing. You come knocking on my door again, I'm going to open it all the way. Understand?"

"Fuck you," Gordo spat.

"That might sound tougher if you weren't laying on the ground with your own piece pressed to your head. But I need you to understand, Gordo. If you come at us again, I will put a bullet through your brains. That's a promise. And I always keep my promises."

"Come on," Nina said, tugging at Brawley's arm, and they hurried off down the street, Brawley holding the pistol at his side and trying to look natural.

They hung a hard left. Brawley stopped long enough to

check the weapon. It was an older Glock knockoff, a single-action Smith & Wesson Sigma 9.

He popped the magazine and pulled back the slide, jacking a round to the macadam. A fucking hollow-point. He released the slide, dry-fired the weapon, and jammed the magazine back into place.

Someone had filed off the serial number. No surprise there.

Texas had reciprocity with Florida and every state in between, so Brawley's permit was good here, but that wouldn't do him any good if he got picked up carrying a black market piece, especially if the pistol in question had ballistics matching open criminal investigations.

The smart move would be to wipe the thing down and drop it into a dumpster, but he felt naked without a firearm. His XDS was across the island in the Winnebago, and the rest of his firearms were back in the Lone Star State. So he shoved the muzzle into his waistband and let his shirt fall over it.

"Shitfuckpissmotherfuckingassholeshit," Nina seethed, tugging him down the alley again. "Fuck, fuck, fuck. We are in deep shit."

Brawley realized then that he was grinning. He hadn't been in a scrap for a while, not since that drunk in Oklahoma had sucker punched him. Hell, that had been a year ago, maybe longer.

"Why are you smiling?" Nina said. "Do you have any idea who that guy was, who he works for?"

"Psi mafia, I'm guessing."

"Exactly, which means, as I was trying to inform you when I realized that you were grinning like a madman, that we are in deep shit."

Brawley shrugged. "I don't know. We could've made out worse. Come on, let's turn onto this street. More people."

They slipped into the flow of foot traffic. It was a beautiful day, and the tourists were out in full force.

The knuckles of Brawley's left hand ached a little, but he didn't think he'd broken anything. Otherwise, he felt fine. Better than fine. Jazzed up, alive, like he'd just ridden a rank bull to the bell and scored 90 plus.

They turned onto Duval Street, where the crowds grew even thicker, people of all ages ambling in happy packs past the shops and bars, everything bright and cheery as a postcard come to life.

Nina calmed down a little. "Gordo's a fuggle. He works for Mr. Dutchman but pals around with Junior."

"So that means Junior and his boys were shaking down the Cat Wizard as a side hustle."

Nina nodded. "If his father finds out, he'll go ballistic."

"So Junior wants to warn you to keep your mouth shut."

"Warn me... or worse. These guys play for keeps."

Brawley felt a twinge of cold rage in his heart. He'd blow the son of a bitch's psionic brains out the back of his skull. "Where is the bastard?"

"Don't even think about it," Nina said. "Junior might look like a douche bag—hell, he is a douche bag—but he's a powerful telekinetic. And really mean."

Brawley let his fingers brush across the pistol hidden in his waistband. "I won't take him lightly."

"This still might blow over," Nina said. "What just happened with Gordo? Junior won't want that getting out. But if we hit Junior, his father will find out and will get involved, and then we would be good and truly fucked. The psi mob has Seekers and technopaths and can call in a Bender if need be. We wouldn't stand a chance. The best thing to do is lay low and hope Junior forgets all about us."

They turned onto Fleming, strolled past a book store and a strip club, and entered a quieter, residential block.

"In the meantime, I'll ask Sage to cloak us," Nina said, slipping her hand into his. "Thanks for pulling my ass out of the fire back there."

Brawley gave her a quick kiss. "Anybody lays a hand on you, darlin, he's going to wish he hadn't."

When they reached the library, Nina started for the steps. "Come on. This is where Sage works."

"Not yet. I still have to check out."

They walked a few more blocks, and he recognized the long porch of Eden House. As they were crossing Fleming, an incredibly loud engine roared to life.

"Oh shit," Nina said, dropping into a crouch beside an airport shuttle idling at the curb. She yanked on Brawley's hand, and he squatted down beside her.

A second later, a black Harley pulled out of the side lot and roared away down the street—but not before Brawley glimpsed the bike's gorgeous, heavily tattooed rider.

"Ugh," Nina said. "Fucking Remi. Texas is sounding better every minute."

"Now you're talking my language, little lady," Brawley said, and they went inside.

"Mr. Hayes," the bearded guy behind the desk said. "A woman was just here looking for you."

"Is that right?" Brawley said. "What did you tell her?"

"Nothing, of course."

"Nothing?"

The man blushed. "Well, almost nothing. She was very... charming. I did tell her that you were staying here, but—"

"She asked for me by name?"

"No," the man said. "She had your picture."

That was curious. "Did you give her my name?"

"No, sir. Of course not."

Brawley and Nina went upstairs. As soon as they entered

his room, Brawley smelled a faint twinge of perfume and motor oil.

"Remi was in here," Nina said.

He nodded. "You smell her, too?"

Nina shook her head and pointed to the bed, where a small, white rectangle lay atop his suitcase.

He crossed the room and picked up the business card.

Between dollar signs and handcuffs, the card read, *Badass Bail Bonds. When you absolutely, positively have to get out of jail tonight. Remington Dupree.*

He flipped the card and saw Remi's personalized message to him: the imprint of her lips in bright red lipstick.

8

B rawley tossed the card and gathered his things. He didn't know whether the guy at the desk had given Remi a key or she'd broken in here. Didn't matter much, one way or the other.

Question was, what the hell did Remi want?

"I'm no Seeker," Nina said, "but I can sense a storm brewing. A shitstorm of epic proportions. You still feeling all lovey dovey toward me, cowboy?"

"I told you," Brawley said. "My feelings won't change. And it's not lovey dovey. It's love. Deal with it."

She smiled, bit her lip, and said, "Let's get out of town before everything blows up."

"Sounds good to me," he said, shouldering his ruck. "My badass RV awaits."

"We have to see my friend Sage first," Nina said. "I'm dying to hear what she says."

"Let's go, then," he said. Opening the door, he scanned the walkway in both directions before stepping from the room. Out in the courtyard, the party was already gearing up, a dozen people boozing it up poolside, another dozen partying in the pool, Buffet playing softly on the speakers.

"I'll have to grab some stuff from my place," she said, then frowned. "And were you serious about me just quitting my job?"

"Darlin'," he said, draping an arm over her shoulders, "do me a favor and start taking me at my word. I say what I mean and mean what I say."

Nina smiled. "You'd better. You have no idea how hard it is to find a job in this town—especially when you're an ex-con."

"Speaking of which, just how much trouble am I taking on here? At exactly which point am I aiding and abetting a criminal, when we cross county lines or just when we leave the state?"

"State. But we don't even have to break county lines. Monroe County stretches all the way up the Keys. I know some people in Marathon and some others in Key Largo. I just have to be back in two weeks to meet with my parole officer. That should give things time to blow over here." Her mismatched eyes flicked back and forth as if she were checking her math. "We have to hang around until afternoon so I can stop by the community center and say goodbye to my little brother, David. He would worry if I didn't."

"Sounds good."

She frowned. "And I have to tell my dad."

"All right. Why the frown?"

"Nothing," she said. "My dad's just a pain in the ass sometimes."

"I haven't met a pretty girl yet whose dad wasn't a pain in the ass. He live around here?"

"Precisely. He lives *around* here. My dad is a professional couch surfer. He likes to keep moving. But I know where to find him once the sun starts to set."

They checked out and started for the library. Brawley kept his eyes peeled. As they walked, Nina explained Sage's order, the Seekers.

Also known as the Order of the Curious, the Seekers were truth mages who dedicated their lives to seeking knowledge. They believed in the Latticework of Truth, an ethereal, four-dimensional network that supposedly connected everything that ever was or would be. Their psionic energy allowed them varying degrees of access to this latticework.

Seekers were walking polygraphs and had the intuition of Gypsy grandmothers. They could read psionic auras, gauge psionic strength in numerical terms, and were experts at unraveling mysteries, solving puzzles, and gathering information. Nina said that some of them were remote viewers.

"What's that?" he asked.

"ESP espionage. They use an inner eye to see stuff happening someplace else."

"So they're like psychic Peeping Toms?"

Nina laughed. "And psychic peeping tomgirls. But most Seekers are harmless. A little batty, maybe. Sometimes, they get obsessed with chasing truth, they just drift away in search of knowledge. It's like they simultaneously have superhuman focus and the worst case of ADD you've ever seen."

"That doesn't make any sense."

Nina grinned. "Neither do Seekers, most of the time. As they get more experienced, they break into two basic groups: the insane and the insanely powerful. The powerhouses can manipulate people's memories, turn invisible, predict the future, all types of crazy shit."

"And the insane ones?"

"They're like chess masters who lose their shit and shun the world to study the game. They become drifters or hole up and go full hermit mode. Quit showering. Nothing matters but information. They get so focused on truth that they lose touch with reality."

"So which type is Sage, crazy or crazy powerful?"

"Neither, yet. She's only twenty-one. But if I had to guess, I'd bet on her getting crazy powerful. Don't get the wrong idea. Sage is awesome. She might seem a little bit out there, but don't be fooled. She's the smartest girl I know. Here we go."

They had reached the library.

Brawley glanced to either side of the steps, half-expecting old Weird Beard to pop out of the foliage, but there was no sign of prophet of destruction.

The Chaotic, he reminded himself.

They entered the library. The main desk was just inside the doors. A friendly looking librarian with dark hair and a goatee greeted them warmly, calling Nina by name.

"Hey, Michael," Nina said. "Is Sage in her cave?"

Michael nodded. "She's ensconced in her realm of dust."

Nina thanked him and led Brawley across the room and rapped on a door that read *Special Collection*. "Sage is the library's historian."

There was no answer.

Nina knocked again, a little harder this time.

The door swung open, and Brawley did his best to keep his mouth from falling open.

The girl who opened the door stood nearly as tall as Brawley. She had the slender physique, long limbs, and elegant neck of a runway model—and a face to match.

She wore stiletto heels, a tight black miniskirt that showed off her shapely legs, and a short-sleeved white blouse complete with a name tag that read *Sage*. Her long blond hair was twisted into a pile atop her head, skewered haphazardly in place by three or four pencils, and still cascaded down her back in a honey-colored waterfall all the way to her ass.

Sage's big, blue eyes regarded Brawley from behind a pair of black-framed glasses that screamed sexy librarian.

"Hey, Sage," Nina said. "This is Brawley."

Sage lifted one golden eyebrow. "That is an unusual name."

Brawley shrugged. "I didn't pick it."

Sage blinked, then wiggled her pixie nose, scrunching her glasses higher up the bridge. "Brawley was not always your name."

"That's news to me," he said. "But I was adopted, so—" He trailed off with a shrug.

Truth be told, the thought kind of rocked him.

Since an early age, he'd known that he was adopted, but it never really mattered to him. Mom and Dad were Mom and Dad. He understood that his birth parents had given him up the same way one might understand that he or she was born at 5:35 in the morning. These were merely interesting tidbits of ancient history signifying nothing.

Somehow, it had never occurred to him that he had been given another name at birth. A strange and oddly powerful notion. Even though it shouldn't really matter, the idea seized onto his thoughts and he couldn't buck it off.

What was his true name?

"Did you wish to see the artifacts?" Sage asked. "We have library cards, letters, and manuscripts from Jimmy Buffet, Shell Silverstein, Ernest Hemingway—"

"Some other time, maybe," Nina interrupted. "We have psi mage questions."

"Nina, I can't talk now," Sage said, turning her back on them and walking into the large room full of bookshelves and filing cabinets.

Brawley couldn't help but notice how tight her ass looked in the black miniskirt.

"I discovered a discrepancy in a shrimper's log from

1947," Sage explained. "The date and day of the week do not match. The shrimper probably just made an error, but I must be certain, so goodbye. Please close the door behind you."

And with no further adieux, the leggy blond librarian disappeared around a tall bookshelf packed not with books but with bundled stacks of paper.

Nina gave Brawley's hand a squeeze, pulled him inside, and closed the door.

"When she said to close the door behind us, I think she meant leave," he said. "As in don't let the door hit you in the ass."

"Like I said, Sage can get lost in her work. As her best friend, it's my job to pull her out now and then. Come on."

On the other side of the shelf, Sage knelt atop a chair with her legs folded under her. She leaned over a rough-looking leather-bound journal, peering through a large magnifying glass. Her glasses were shoved up into her blond hair, loose tresses of which corkscrewed down onto the table. As she leaned forward, her tight-looking ass strained against the fabric of her short skirt, which had hiked all the way to the top of her thighs.

"Sage, we really need to talk to you."

Sage flinched, obviously startled, then turned slowly until one blue eye regarded Nina impatiently. She gritted a pencil in her teeth like a pirate biting down on a knife blade. Withdrawing the pencil, Sage said, "As I already explained, Nina, this is not a convenient time. This journal is—"

Grinning like a madwoman, Nina reached out and touched the librarian's shoulder. "That shit can wait, girlfriend. This is big. Seriously. It's going to blow your mind."

"You have ten seconds to convince me."

Nina launched into a stumbling, breathless explanation. "Last night, I fucked Brawley and opened his strand, and this big loop of energy connected us, and now I feel super powerful, and he located his strand on the first try, and he already started drawing power, and I think I'm going crazy because I feel like I'm in love with him, and I need you to look at his aura, because something crazy is going on, and we're leaving town today because the psi mafia wants to kill us, so you have to help us now not later, please."

The golden eyebrow arched again. Sage laid the magnifying glass on the open journal and put her glasses on again. Then she twitched her nose, apparently adjusting their position.

She unfolded her long legs, got down from the chair, and approached Brawley. She stared at him for a second. Then, for several seconds, she seemed to stare through him, her eyes losing focus.

When her eyes returned, she blinked at him, tilting her head like a quizzical dog.

"Hmm," Sage said. "Your aura is strange."

Brawley spread his hands. "Like Nina said, twenty-four hours ago, I didn't know shit about psionics."

Sage shook her head. "That is inconsequential. Even as infants, psi mages radiate perceptibly. And once the strand opens, your full aura is visible to Seekers. But I needed several seconds of intense focus to detect your aura. Initially, I had the distinct impression that you were not psionic gifted. But then, when your power shone through…"

Sage turned to Nina. "I see what you mean about his power. I have never seen a psi score this high. 166."

Nina's jaw dropped.

To Brawley, Sage said, "You throb with power. Once you learn to harness your energy, you will be truly formidable."

"You're a rock star," Nina said, giving him a playful shove. Then she turned to Sage. "But what's so weird about his aura?"

"Despite its potency, his aura is incomplete," Sage said.

She looked at Brawley and frowned. "Nina's aura is a sphere of red light since she's an Unbound. My own aura is a yellow sphere since I'm a Seeker. Yours is red and spherical, as it should be, but most of the sphere's surface is missing. There's a swath of red here," she said, swiping her finger through the air. Then she slashed her finger at a downward angle. "A stripe here." She drew a circle in the air. "A swirl there. It's like your sphere is invisible, and only a small portion of it—say fifteen percent—is showing through."

Brawley didn't know what to think of that. "Is this a problem?"

Sage crossed her thin arms over her chest, screwed up her face with concentration, and exhaled, stirring an errant lock of blond hair that had fallen across her beautiful face. "No. I mean, you're already super powerful. But… why does your aura look like a mesh ball? Do you mind if I check something?"

He shrugged. "Go for it."

Sage reached out and laid her hand on his chest. Her fingers were long and slender. She wore no fingernail polish, and the nails were chewed to the quick. But even the telltale ravages of anxiety couldn't deter from the beautiful perfection of those fingers, just as her lack of makeup made her face no less beautiful.

As she touched him, her eyelids fluttered.

Nina sat on the table top, watching with intense curiosity.

Sage's eyes opened wide. "That is extremely interesting. Someone cloaked you a long time ago."

"What's that mean?"

"A cloak creates a screen," Sage said.

"Psi camo," Nina chimed in.

"Yes," Sage agreed. "Which explains the initial difficulty I encountered when attempting to perceive your aura, despite focused effort. A vicinity scan or even a standard aura check would detect nothing."

"Who would've cloaked me?" Brawley said. "And why?"

"Unfortunately, I am not powerful enough to determine those answers." She frowned, narrowing her eyes thoughtfully. "I really want to know. The cloak is unusually strong. Someone went to extreme lengths to protect you from discovery."

"You said it's been in place for a long time," Nina said. "I'll bet his birth mother did it. Or father, I guess. Maybe one of his parents was a psi mage, the other wasn't, and the psionic parent didn't want to live their life hiding the truth from the other, so they put a cloak on Brawley to protect him from detection and gave him up for adoption to some norms."

"That is pure conjecture," Sage said, "and highly unlikely. Brawley is Unbound, after all, and only a powerful Seeker could have created this cloak."

"So his mom was Unbound and his dad was a Seeker," Nina said with a so-what shrug. "My dad's a telepath, and my mom was obviously Unbound, though the only trick she ever showed me was how to disappear."

Brawley let her know he didn't understand.

"My mom walked out on me when I was a newborn," Nina said, and held up a hand. "But do me a favor and don't say you're sorry, because I hate sympathy with a passion."

Brawley just gave her a nod. He could understand that. He'd never had much use for sympathy himself. It didn't do any damn good, and most of the time, it was really about the sympathizer, not the one suffering.

"So his parents were both psi mages," Nina said, "but they gave him up for one reason or another and didn't want the psi community in his business. The question is, why?"

"Why, indeed," Sage said. She stood there nibbling a fingernail for a second, staring through Brawley, clearly lost in thought. Then her hand dropped from her mouth, and her blue eyes went huge behind the lenses of her glasses. Sage was a pale girl—probably both from her natural complexion and from spending too much time inside reading books, Brawley figured—but what little color she had drained from her awestruck face, leaving her white as milk. "How old are you?"

"Twenty-three."

Sage laughed nervously, frowned, glanced at Nina, who looked just as clueless as Brawley felt, then swung her eyes back to Brawley. When she spoke, she sounded both excited and frightened. "I am curious. What is your birthday?"

"January 9th."

Sage let out a shuddering breath. "That is remarkable."

Nina popped off the table and hurried over. In unison, she and Brawley asked, "What?"

Sage didn't answer immediately. Her eyes flicked side to side. She stood there wringing her hands, mumbling to herself, clearly wrestling with her thoughts. "Pure conjecture... but the date... the sphere, the *power...*"

Watching her, Brawley remembered Nina talking about how Seekers were a little crazy. Right now, Sage looked nuttier than a five-pound fruit cake.

Sage quit mumbling, nodded, and lifted her chin to stare in Brawley's eyes for a second. She bit her lip and then turned to Nina. "We might be standing on the brink of a big discovery. A huge discovery, in fact."

"What are you talking about?" Nina asked.

"The evidence suggests," Sage said, then broke off, laughing and shaking her pretty head. "Okay, I shouldn't really call it evidence, but..."

Sage went to a desk heaped in books and papers. Shoving a stack of yellowed newspapers aside, she pulled a landline phone from the clutter. She picked up the receiver, held it to her ear, and pushed a button. Then she stood there, chewing a fingernail and shimmying back and forth like she needed to pee.

"Michael, it's Sage. I'm taking an early lunch, okay? Yes, I'm still here, but pretend I'm not, okay? Thank you."

Turning back toward Brawley and Sage, she said, "We have to check. I *must* know the truth."

Brawley and Nina exchanged confused looks.

Sage crossed the room to the door, threw the bolt, and turned to face them.

"Take off your clothes, please, Brawley," Sage said, and started unbuttoning her blouse.

9

"Hold on now," Brawley said, watching as the slender blond librarian opened her blouse, revealing a long, lean, small-breasted body too feminine to be called athletic. His original impression still rang true as she dropped the blouse to the ground, standing before him in only heels, the tight black miniskirt, and a lacy white bra; Sage was built for the catwalk.

Which was hot. And his dick was responding. Big time. Ever since getting with Nina, his body had coursed with vitality, and even after a night of nearly constant sex, he'd been hornier than a three-peckered billy goat all day.

But that was only his body. And he hadn't been kidding when he'd told Nina he loved her. He wasn't about to ruin what he had with Nina, even if Sage looked like a super model and sexy librarian all rolled into one. Right now, Sage was bent at the waist with one hip cocked, both hands fiddling at the small of her back, unzipping the miniskirt.

With effort, Brawley dragged his eyes from this gorgeous lunatic and turned to Nina.

Who, he was shocked to see, had already peeled off her

tank top. Her magnificent breasts wobbled as she unzipped her shorts. "What are you waiting for, cowboy? You heard the girl."

"I take it you're okay with this," he said. He didn't know exactly what was happening here, but it seemed like Sage wanted to do more than reorganize the card catalog. Part of him—most of him—wanted Nina to say yes. But another part —the loving, fiercely possessive part of him that had come so powerfully to life in the night—remained concerned that doing something with Sage might change things between them. Brawley was far from timid, but he'd been laid enough to know that love was worth more than even the finest piece of ass in the universe.

"Yeah," Nina said. "I don't really know what she has in mind, but it sounds like she's trying to figure out something about you. Something huge. She never exaggerates, so it must be a really big deal. I trust her. You should, too."

"I think she wants me to do more than trust her," Brawley said. Glancing at Sage, he saw her coming their way dressed only in heels, lacy white panties, a matching bra, and her sexy-ass glasses.

"Well, I hope she wants to do a lot more," Nina said. She popped onto her tiptoes and gave him a quick kiss. Her firm cleavage brushed across his arm. "Don't worry. Whatever this is, it's not going to change what we have."

"So says the girl that laughed when I said I love her," Brawley said.

Nina rolled her eyes. "Didn't you hear me tell Sage the same thing? I love you, too. Okay? It just felt weird saying it. And let's just get everything out in the open." She reached up to hold his face in her hands, and her mismatched eyes stared deep into his. "I'm not looking for an open relation- ship. You are my man—the only man I want. But if Sage wants to play with us, I'm fine with that. More than fine.

Whatever happened between us last night, Brawley, it changed me, changed us, bound us in some deep, psionic way. Don't make me tell you everything I feel right now, okay?"

Nina laughed. "It's embarrassing. I'm supposed to be tough and independent, jaded even, and all I want to do is make you happy. Enough, enough. I don't want to say anything else, okay? If you're not comfortable with this situation, fine, but I am, and I need you to know that no matter what happens here, I am yours and yours alone for as long as you'll have me."

Brawley nodded.

Nina pulled the pistol from his waistband and set it on a cart of books. Then she grabbed his erection, and a playful grin lit her face. "Now quit playing bashful and get out of these clothes, cowboy."

Brawley laughed and leaned in to kiss her. Nina gripped his face in her hands and kissed him with wild passion, her tongue busy in his mouth, her breath going ragged. He could feel her urgency.

Together, they stripped off his clothes as Sage stood there watching. "Oh," the librarian said, and her eyes bulged, staring at his manhood. "Your penis is rather large."

Nina laughed. "It's a good thing you're so hot, Sage, because your game is lame. 'Your dick is so huge' sounds better."

"Semantics," Sage said. "Take off your panties but leave on your stockings and boots. They are strangely appealing."

"Really?" Nina said, looking down at herself and shimmying out of her tiny black panties. Her incredible body was stark naked save for her garter belt, fishnet stockings, and combat boots.

"Yes," Brawley said, "really." His dick was harder than Chuck Norris.

"Thanks, babe," Nina said. "Okay, Sage, what is this all about?"

"Searching for the truth," Sage said.

"In that case, you came to the right place," Nina said, grabbing Brawley by the shaft. "Because let me tell you, this is the truth."

"Please kneel down and put his penis in your mouth," Sage said. She held one skinny forearm across her narrow waist, just above the pronounced hip bones. The other hand raised to her lips, where she chewed a nail, watching with keen interest as Nina lowered her knees to the floor.

Holding him in both hands, Nina positioned her lips inches from his throbbing member. "I'm not doing it unless you tell me right."

Sage rolled her eyes. "Don't be childish, Nina. This is serious business. I don't want to reveal my hypothesis—there is too much circumstantial evidence involved—but if my suspicions prove correct, we are about to make an historic discovery. Now, do your part so that I can study your auras as you fellate him."

"Fellate?" Nina laughed. "You make it sound like I'm blowing up a balloon. And I'm not blowing anything until you say it right."

"Fine," Sage sighed, brushing the air with an impatient get-on-with-it gesture. "Suck his dick, Nina. Okay? Suck his huge cock, you filthy slut. Better?"

"Much," Nina said, and plunged her warm mouth over the swollen head of his manhood. It was too big and thick for her to fit more than a few inches in her mouth but not for a lack of trying.

"Interesting," Sage said. "Very interesting indeed."

"Yeah, it is," Brawley said, looking back and forth between the two women.

Nina looked impossibly hot kneeling below him, eyes

closed, lips stretched tight around his girth as her head bobbed up and down. Her tits looked incredible, and Sage was right about the stockings and boots. There was something oddly sexy about the combination—though nothing could be sexier than Nina's soft moans and the wet sounds coming from where her free hand worked feverishly between her legs.

The scene quickened something in Brawley, that part of him that had first manifested the previous night. He felt not just powerful but dominant, and it excited him, looking down at his beautiful woman serving him on her knees.

"I am going to touch both of you now," Sage said, and her weird clinical announcement was surprisingly sexy in juxtaposition to Nina's unbridled passion.

Sage stepped close. She settled one hand on the back of Nina's bobbing head, and the fingertips of her other hand pressed lightly into Brawley's abdomen just above his appendectomy scar.

"Most fascinating," Sage said, as if the three of them were gathered around a microscope instead of acting out a scene from some library fetish flick. "Nina, your aura is much stronger than it used to be."

"Mmhm," Nina agreed, still going at it.

"And your psi score has risen," Sage said, her voice incredulous.

"Mmhm?" Nina repeated, this time with an inquisitive inflection.

"This shouldn't be possible," Sage said. "For as long as I've known you, your score has been 140. But somehow it has risen ten percent to 154."

Nina popped her mouth free. "Fuck yeah," she panted. "I told you he'd done something to me. 154 is high, right?"

Sage nodded, looking amazed. "Fewer than one psi mage in 2700 have a score that high. That means you're more powerful than all but a few hundred psi mages in the United States."

"Sweet," Nina said, and started sucking Brawley again.

"Your auras have bound," Sage said, her voice trembling with awe. "Wherever they intersect, your energies have braided together. Just as they would if…"

Sage stepped back and jerked down her lacy, white panties. "I have to know the truth," she said, untangling her heels from the panties. "Brawley, please insert your penis in my vagina."

Brawley laughed.

So did Nina, though her laughter was muffled at first. She popped her mouth free and said, "You know the drill, sister. If you want my man to do you, say it right."

Sage gave an exasperated sigh. "This isn't the time for games, Nina. We might be on the verge of an incredible discovery, and the only way to determine the truth is for Brawley to insert his—"

"No," Nina interrupted. "If you want it, say—"

"Fuck me, Brawley," Sage said, not putting much into it. "Please fuck me with your huge cock. Okay?"

"Works for me," Brawley said, moving forward.

"Now, what would be the most efficient way to do this?" Sage wondered aloud, raising a knuckle to her pretty lips.

"To hell with that," Nina said. "This is fucking, not calculus."

She grabbed her skinny friend by the arm, dragged her across the room, and bent her over the table facing away from Brawley. Nina positioned her with her hands on the table and her feet spread apart, as if Sage was about to be frisked and cuffed alongside a cop car.

Brawley watched, surging with desire. It was all he could do not to snort like a bull.

Nina slapped Sage's pretty bottom. "Now stick out that

pretty little ass of yours and get ready for the biggest dick of your life."

Sage bent her knees a little, lowering her tight little ass and pushing it out. "I am prepared."

Nina propped one leg onto the table, fingering herself wetly as she watched them with gleaming eyes. "Fuck her, Brawley," she panted.

Brawley grabbed Sage's ass in both hands. He was an ass man and loved Nina's juicy peach of a bottom, but as far as smaller asses went, Sage's was perfect, high and tight and muscular but still beautifully curved. It was the ass of a Victoria's Secret model.

He growled with appreciation, then ran his hands up her sides, over the rumble strips of her prominent ribs. Apparently, Sage wasn't ticklish because she didn't so much as giggle. He moved in close behind her, pinning his throbbing erection between his abdomen and her ass, and reached around to fill his hands with her breasts. He could feel the shape of her small, firm mounds through the lacy fabric, but he didn't want to just feel the shape of them. He wanted to touch her flesh.

He shoved his fingers under the bra. Her tits were small and firm, the nipples tiny and hard.

"Please insert your penis," Sage said, her voice sounding almost conversational. "I am very excited to learn the truth."

"I'll show you the truth," he said. Standing straight, he reached between her legs.

For all of Sage's robotic matter-of-factness, her sex was swollen and soaked with excitement. Whether that excitement was due to him or her curiosity, he didn't give a damn.

Because he decided there and then to fuck the composure straight out of this businesslike librarian.

He gave her tight ass three good slaps with his hardness then shoved it straight into her wet mound, burying his entire length in her slick channel, which gripped him tightly.

"Oh!" Sage cried out, and the surprise in her voice and hitch in her breath spurred him on, stoking the dominant beast swelling within him.

He drew back his hips and slammed them forward, and Sage cried out again. "Your penis is quite large."

Brawley grabbed a handful of her long, golden hair, twisted it around his grip, and hauled back like it was a bull rope.

Sage yelped with surprise.

Brawley started slamming away, pounding this beautiful, casually aloof beauty with every inch of his manhood. Neither one of them had an ounce of fat on their bodies, and when their flesh met, it slapped crisply together. With every pounding thrust, Brawley plunged deep, burying his throbbing pole in her tight sex. And with ever slap of their flesh, Sage cried out. Soon she was breathing hard, then panting, then grunting and growling in a most undignified manner.

It was a huge turn-on, breaking her out of her clinical nature, bringing out the human in her, and Brawley would have surrendered to the dominant beast swelling within him and started pounding even harder, but then something happened—something so surprising that it hauled his attention away from breaking this gorgeous supermodel.

His dick was glowing again. His dick and balls and abdomen. And so were Sage's loins.

He was feeling with her what he had felt when Nina opened his strand, only the sensation of burgeoning euphoria was even more intense this time. A second later, he understood why.

Nina's moaning was the only clue he needed.

He glanced at his love. Nina was transfixed with pleasure

—head thrown back, mouth open, eyes shut—trembling as she clamped both hands over her pulsing sex.

Watching her, he felt a staggering surge of affection, possessiveness, and pure, unbridled, white-hot lust.

And that's when he realized why the incredible sensation spreading away from his union with Sage was so powerful. He could feel Nina, too!

Apparently, Nina could feel him as well. "Yes," she groaned. "Oh, yes. That's incredible. Oh you feel so good, Brawley. And Sage, you feel amazing."

"As do you," Sage said, her voice choppy from the hard fucking Brawley continued to give her. "I can feel you both. It is quite unusual."

"Fuck us, Brawley," Nina begged. "Fuck us hard, babe."

Releasing Sage's hair, Brawley seized her narrow hips and threw his back into it, pounding away savagely as the pulsing energy spread, flooding all three of their bodies with rapturous energy.

Brawley laughed, drunk on happiness and this unbelievable surge of power. His energy had somehow bound to the psionic essence of both women, and once again, feelings of affection and protectiveness and dominance rose in him, magnifying his emotions toward Nina and hauling Sage into his heart as well.

Which made no sense, of course.

He'd just met Sage. Didn't know her at all. And she was an odd girl. It wasn't possible that he—

Brawley laughed again, crushing those weak-ass objections. He adored this sexy librarian, and she was his now. His and his alone forever. They had all the time in the world to get to know each other.

With every crisp slap of his flesh against hers, this warmth and excitement grew stronger.

"Most unusual," Sage's shaky voice stuttered. "Most pleasurable. Something is—uhn!"

"Yes!" Nina gasped.

A tidal wave of psionic energy blasted through their bodies burst from their heads. Rivers of power flowed through the threesome, connecting their minds and loins.

This time, Brawley could see the crackling strands, which braided together two distinct energies, one bright red, the other brilliant yellow.

"Oh my damn!" Nina cried, and Sage chimed in with an uncharacteristic yodel of wordless elation that somehow managed to voice the joy, lust, power, and wonderment coursing through the trio.

Then Sage thrust hard with her mind, pouring her psionic vitality into them. The yellow strand flashed with blinding brightness, and Brawley roared as a fracture in his mind blasted wide open.

Their bodies fucked madly as their minds slammed together in a thoughtless mosh pit of pleasure and power until the threesome cried out as one, vaporized by a nuclear explosion of mutual orgasm.

After much bucking and moaning, the bands of power uncoupled, whipping away in three separate sections. A flash of red energy rushed into Nina. Crackling yellow light disappeared into Sage. And a red and yellow barber's pole plunged into Brawley.

His body shuddered as these braided energies rushed through him, exploded in his skull, and crushed down into a single point that snapped away into some secret capacitor in his mind.

"What the fuck?" Nina gasped, collapsing to the ground. "What the fuck?"

Even in his confusion and elation, Brawley had to grin at the way her stunned utterances echoed her reactions to their first coupling. He leaned over Sage's quivering body and kissed her pale back.

Sage turned her face sideways, trying to see Brawley. A veil of golden hair had fallen over her face and undulated now with her panting breath.

"What the fuck?" Nina moaned nearby.

Brawley reached down, gently brushed Sage's blond hair aside, and straightened her glasses, which had gone cockeyed.

Her blue eyes stared at him with something like awe. "You," she panted. "You are a power mage."

10

"Huh?" Brawley said.

"Wait... what?" Nina said, rising shakily to her feet. Rattled by ecstasy and gleaming with perspiration, she looked amazing.

Brawley pulled his length from Sage's slick heat and pointed it in the direction of his love.

His *first* love, that was.

Because sensible or otherwise, the adoration he now felt toward this golden-haired stranger could be nothing other than love. He did not feel for Sage what he felt for Nina—how could he?—but he wouldn't try to deny the glowing ember of affection that was certain to shortly ignite into a blaze of true love.

"It is as I suspected," Sage said, wobbling as she stood on shaky legs. "Or rather, it is as I had not fully allowed myself to suspect. It seemed so improbable."

"Improbable?" Nina said. "You mean impossible. The power mages are dead."

Sage shook her head. "They are dead no longer." She gestured toward Brawley. "He just opened a second strand

and bound the three of us together. Our lover is a power mage, the first power mage in twenty-three years."

"Oh shit," Nina said. "We are fucked."

"Speaking of which," Brawley said, touching the delicious curve of her sweaty hip.

Nina skittered away as if he'd touched her with a curling iron. "Oh no you don't, mister. Keep that ball bat away from me. I need a minute to recover, and this shit Sage is talking about, it's a big deal. A huge deal. Epically huge. Like *we are totally screwed, everything is changed forever, what the fuck is Nina supposed to do now* huge."

"Meanwhile, I'm just standing here with my dick in my hand and no clue what y'all are talking about," Brawley said.

"When Nina described her experiences with you, I began to speculate on the possibility," Sage said, straightening her lacy white bra. "Then you told me your age, and I had to investigate. Twenty-three years ago, the Order orchestrated a mass execution known as the Culling. In one fell swoop, the Order killed every power mage on Earth."

As Sage spoke, Brawley felt a surge of curiosity. He was riveted to her words. He had to understand this, had to know the truth.

"The Order explained that the Culling was done to protect the psi community," Sage explained.

"Bullshit," Nina interrupted. "My dad says it was a power grab."

"Whatever the case," Sage said, bending to step into her panties, "the Order determined that power mages were too strong—and too dangerous—to live." She turned to Brawley. "Normal psionicists are limited to a single strand of power. No matter how powerful we become, we will never gain access to other strands."

Sage twitched her pixie nose and smiled. "You increased my psi score by ten percent to 145. Thank you. This will be quite advantageous in my studies. But I remain a Seeker and will always be limited to the talents of my order. Nina will likewise remain limited to the abilities of the Unbound."

Sage focused on Nina for a second and said, "Bonding with me raised your psi score to 157."

"Hot damn," Nina said with a grin. "Another two percent boost. I'm anxious to see what, exactly, that means. You two pumped me full of so much energy, I feel like a volcano ready to erupt. What's our all mighty lover's psi score now?"

Sage looked at Brawley, blinked, and smiled again. "169."

"Cool," Brawley said, recognizing the high number even if he couldn't even draw a strand yet. "But what do these scores mean, exactly? Are they like a power bar on a video game."

"Yeah," Nina said. "Like mana, if you know what I mean."

Brawley nodded. He'd never gone in much for video games. Like all other complicated electronics, he was pretty much allergic to them. But the cowboys he'd traveled with played them all the time.

"Having a lot of juice lets you do more stuff," Nina said. "Every psionic action burns up juice. Some more than others. And some actions, you can choose to open the throttle and pour in more force. So if I wanted to do something simple, like…" she paused, glanced at the book cart, and the pistol lifted into the air and floated over to Brawley, "…hand you your gun, I'd only burn a point or two. There's not an exact point cost per action, but you get the idea."

He nodded. "So each action has a cost."

"Yes, if I decided to pick up Sage's desk and hurl it across the room—"

"Please don't," Sage said. "My desk might not look orga-nized, but I assure you that I know the location of every item, right down to the smallest Post-It note."

"I don't doubt it, Brainiac," Nina said, "and you can chill. I'm not going to wreck your weird-ass lair. But if I did throw the desk, it might burn fifty or sixty points. Again, I'm ballparking, but you probably get what I'm saying."

"Also," Sage added, "though one's psi score is supposed to remain fixed from birth to death, it is not the sole determiner of one's functional power. If you are focused, train hard, secure a knowledgeable mentor, and concentrate on efficiency of technique, you can learn to spend fewer points per action."

Sage glanced at Nina and said, "So an experienced, hard-working psi mage born with a psi score in the low 130s might, over time, learn to perform so efficiently that she could execute more psionic actions between rest periods than, say, her dear friend who was lucky enough to be born with a higher score but who never put in the effort to maximize her potential."

"Yeah, yeah, yeah," Nina said, and stuck her tongue out at Sage.

"Works for me," Brawley said. "Practice is my middle name."

"No it isn't," Nina said. "Your middle name is Peckinpah."

"You're a funny one," Brawley said, and mussed her purple hair. "So what you're telling me is, as a power mage, I can tap more than one strand?"

"Yes," Sage said. "In fact, you already have. Perhaps you already feel an unusual degree of curiosity?"

He nodded.

"As I suspected," Sage said. "And you feel an illogically potent affection toward me?"

He nodded again.

Sage smiled. It seemed spontaneous and girlish and made her pretty in a new way that dinged a little bell in Brawley's heart. "I feel the same way toward you," she said. Then, turning to Nina, she added. "And toward you."

"Aw, thanks," Nina said, and embraced her friend. "I love you, too, Sage."

Something primal and hungry rose in Brawley as he watched Sage's pale abdomen crush up against Nina's spherical breasts.

"Of course you do," Sage said happily. "We are bound. All three of us are bound together, thanks to our power mage."

Standing arm in arm, the two women smiled at Brawley.

His mind was racing along, wanting answers. "So Nina, why did you seem so upset when Sage said I was a power mage?"

Nina frowned. "Because we are fucked. You're not supposed to exist, Brawley. Twenty-three years ago, the Order didn't orchestrate a pruning. It was a Culling. And when they find out that you're a power mage, they're going to finish the job."

"Oh no," Sage said, looking suddenly terrified. "I have been so elated that I didn't realize…"

"What?"

"An event this significant will resonate across the Latticework of Truth. Even as we speak, Seekers are receiving some sense of what has happened here. I don't think anyone will be able to see Brawley specifically, not in the initial resonance, but we have to cloak you. Seekers the world over are likely trying to uncover your identity at this very moment."

"I thought you said I was cloaked already."

"Just wait," Nina said. "Let Sage do her thing."

Sage reached out and placed a hand on Brawley's forehead. "Physical contact isn't strictly necessary, but it will strengthen the obscuring shroud."

As she spoke, Brawley felt a strange, tickling sensation in his head, as if a light shawl of feathers was settling overtop his mind.

"Oh," Sage said, sounding surprised and happy. "This new

power you've given me is quite impressive. Normally, cloaking someone would have taken extreme concentration and would have left me exhausted. But it was easy, and I feel completely fine. This makes me very curious about my potential."

"That's it, then?" Brawley asked. "I'm protected?"

Sage nodded. "As well as I can protect you, anyway. We can't take any chances, though. If my order suspects that a new power mage has emerged, they will scour the Lattice-work night and day, hunting for any clue about your identity or whereabouts. They likely already know our general location. Not precisely, but they probably understand that we are in Florida, perhaps even the Keys. They might even suspect Key West."

"Yeah," Nina said. "About that, the *we* part, do the Seekers know about you and me?"

"Not me," Sage said. "I am always cloaked. You, though? Doubtful. But we can't be too careful." She reached out, placed a hand on Nina's forehead, and a second later pronounced the Unbound beauty to be cloaked.

"Sweet," Nina said. "Thanks."

Shimmying into her skirt, Sage said, "Unfortunately, I am only capable of a simple cloaking at this point. With this new power, I should be able to learn stronger cloaking feats quickly, but we need to visit Hazel tonight."

"Is that your crazy mentor?" Nina said.

Sage frowned. "Hazel is not insane. She is very powerful and perhaps a touch eccentric, but—"

"The hammock lady, right?"

"Yes, Hazel enjoys lying in her—"

"Crazy," Nina said. "As in batshit, cuckoo bananas crazy. Which assures me that we are totally fucked."

"We need Hazel's help," Sage said, slipping into her blouse. "Besides, she might be able to help Brawley figure out the mystery of his past. This revelation explains the powerful cloaking spell you've been carrying all these years. One of your parents was apparently a power mage. Either they sensed the Culling, which occurred on the day you were born, and cloaked you in advance of the tragedy, or your mother survived long enough to cloak and hide you. Hazel might be able to tell us, and she might be able to determine who your parents were, as well."

Brawley was burning with curiosity, but Sage needed to get back to work. They agreed to meet after her shift. In the meantime, Brawley and Nina would go back to her place, grab a few things, and visit her brother and father before heading across the island to Brawley's RV.

Sage would put in for an emergency leave of absence, and tonight, after they spoke with Hazel, the three of them would leave Key West together, just in case the Seekers—and by extension, the Order—determined the basic location of the event. Because if the Latticework coalesced around Key West, the island would soon be crawling with Seekers, Order agents, and perhaps even FPI agents.

"Federal Paranormal Investigations," Nina explained as they left the library.

It was surprisingly difficult for Brawley to say goodbye to Sage. Yes, he barely knew her, but he wanted to know her, and furthermore, he hated leaving her here alone, even if she was almost certainly safe. These psionic bonds of love were awesome but obviously came with a price. He would never again be truly carefree, not unless his women were safely by his side.

As they walked out, Michael waved goodbye, grinning in a way that told Brawley that the friendly librarian had gotten an earful of lewd sounds through the bolted door.

Brawley automatically started to lift his hand to tip his

hat in farewell, remembered again that he no longer wore one, and gave the guy a parting wave instead.

"The FPI is always snooping around, looking for us," Nina said. "And when something big happens, they always seem to know about it. Word on the street is they keep Seekers in some government dungeon and force them to do psionic surveillance."

Brawley listened intently, still seized by a fever of curiosity. There was so much he wanted to know. What did it mean to be a power mage? Who were his parents? What was his true name?

A tornado of questions swirled in his mind. He wanted to know everything, especially everything about the psionic community. That went double for his past and quadruple for anything that might pose a threat to his women.

All this being said, he still forced himself to scan their surroundings. It wouldn't do to walk blindly into an ambush.

"So the FPI is part of the government?" he asked. "As in the fuggle government, not the Order?"

"That's correct" Nina said. "Your hard-earned tax dollars at work in the world."

"How come I've never heard of them, then?"

Nina laughed. "You think the government wants voters to know they're funding investigations into paranormal events? The FPI keeps a low profile and a lower budget. As far the bureaus go, the FPI is definitely the ugly runt of the litter. They're thinly staffed and underequipped, and from what I hear, their home office is an abandoned missile silo in the Midwest. According to my dad, the place looks like the lobby of a one-star motel and smells like mildew and coffee. The FPI agents still use the beat-up, black vans they were issued a million years ago. They look like they drove straight off the pages of *Firestarter*."

"They sound like a joke."

"Yeah, but don't let their cheap suits and sketchy rides fool you. What they lack in funding, they make up for in persistence. These people are serious. I mean dedicated to the cause. They're like modern day crusaders. And they will stop at nothing to find us and lock us in cages."

When they turned onto Duval Street, Brawley's stomach roared like a lion. He nodded toward a place called Willie T's, where people sat outside eating burgers and fries, drinking beer, and listening to a live band play what sounded like a cross between rock and jazz.

"Let's go to my place first," Nina said. "I want to get my shit before Junior Dutchman sends someone to welcome me home."

Brawley bristled at the thought of someone meaning Nina harm. "I still say I just cut to the chase, track down this asshole, and shoot him between the eyes."

Nina gave his arm a squeeze. "Easy, tiger. How about we just lay low, get out of here with Sage tonight, and spend the next couple of weeks playing cards and having sex."

Brawley grinned. "That sounds pretty good, too."

When they reached her street, he told her to hang back while he investigated.

She laughed at that. "You have no idea how powerful I feel right now."

"Cool," he said. "But hold up and let me go first."

"All right," she said, trailing several feet behind him while he investigated the alley beside her place. Nina's pink moped was still chained by the fence. Brawley paused there, listening for a moment and scanning the ground near the fence gate.

Everything was sand and gravel here. He couldn't even make out their own tracks, let alone cut for sign.

He stretched onto his tiptoes and looked over the fence. The backyard was empty. A slight breeze corrugated the surface of the pool, upon which a few stray leaves spun like rudderless boats.

Boats about to sink, Brawley thought.

Then he paused, wondering where the hell that thought had come from. He had no idea, but a sense of deep foreboding washed over him.

He slipped the pistol from his waistband, racked the slide, and held the weapon alongside his leg, making it less obvious to any nosey neighbor who might be peeking between the curtains.

The sense of foreboding remained, a vague yet powerful warning echoing over and over in his mind like the instinctive warning call of some primordial beast that had taken up residence within his skull.

Meanwhile, he felt a faint prickling sensation in his head, as if the inside of his skull was itching.

"What is it?" Nina whispered, stepping up beside him.

"Don't know," he whispered. "Just got a gut feeling that something isn't right here."

She tugged at his arm. "We can't ignore that. Sage opened your Seeker strand, and Seekers have a gift for smelling trouble."

He nodded. It made sense, and his gut was kicking him in the ass, trying to hustle him out of there. At the same time, he wrestled with his curiosity. He wanted to know what the hell was going on here. And if there was a threat, if someone was waiting for Nina, well, he wanted to go in there and snap their fucking necks.

But that would be stupid. They would have the drop on him.

"Come on," she said, tugging his arm again. "I'll get that shit later, when we come back to town. It's not worth it."

"All right," he said, kicking his curiosity and anger to the curb and turning with her to go.

Then, with a loud squeal, a dark blur turned into the driveway and roared straight at them.

Instantly, even as his body was still reacting to the threat, Brawley's mind recognized the black Escalade from their earlier run-in with the psi mob.

The driver stomped the accelerator. The SUV lurched, roaring like a monster, and rushed straight at them. The wide grille gleamed, stretching all the way across the narrow drive from fence to fence.

Brawley grabbed Nina, meaning to shoulder through the gate and haul her to safety, but Nina gave an angry cry and thrust her hand forward in the direction of the onrushing vehicle.

With a loud smashing sound, the SUV slammed to a crunching stop. Its ass end hopped into the air. The grille folded and the hood buckled. A hulking man in a blue and silver track suit smashed through the passenger side of the tinted windshield, skipped off the hood, and crashed into the gravel path.

A geyser of steam erupted from the ruined hood, but not before Brawley made out a figure in the driver's seat, struggling with his seat belt, and detected someone else moving in the second row.

Brawley raised the Smith & Wesson and fired three shots at the driver, then snapped off three more, raking the cabin. The erupting radiator made it impossible to judge the effectiveness of his shooting.

Nina called to him from where she had opened the gate, but Brawley waved her off and rushed the Escalade, staying low. He'd never been in a shootout before, but if life had taught him one lesson it was to see things through.

When the world started bucking, you had to grab hold and ride to the fucking bell.

He ran around the passenger side, cursing himself for not

counting his ammo. Most of these 9mm Glock knockoffs held at least ten rounds.

The backdoor popped open, and a skinny guy with a line of blood running down his forehead leaned out, shouted something in Spanish, and cut loose with an automatic weapon.

Brawley fired two quick shots.

The guy jerked, stitching the sky with gunfire, and crumpled in a twitching heap to the gravel beside the Escalade.

Brawley fired again, drilling another hole through the bastard for good measure. The guy didn't so much as yelp.

Hunching low, Brawley slid along the fender. Still moving, he lifted his hand level with the front passenger window, squeezed off two quick shots into the cabin, shoulder checked the rear door shut, and dove over the fallen man.

Gunfire exploded within the vehicle, punching holes through the door Brawley had just closed.

Scooping up the dead man's machine pistol, Brawley checked to make sure Nina was nowhere in sight then hooked around the back of the Cadillac and hosed it down with lead, burning through the rest of the magazine, smashing out the windows and hopefully killing every last motherfucker in there.

For several seconds, there was no sign of movement from his attackers. In the distance, a siren began to wail, and Brawley figured there was about a 99% chance it was heading this way.

They had to get out of there.

Then the Escalade rocked, and there was a creaking sound as the rear passenger door opened.

Brawley saw someone limping toward the rear of the SUV and heard ragged breathing. He waited for a clean shot. First, he saw the bloody hand gripping a pistol. Then the arm. Then a man covered in blood lurched around the vehicle, moving jerkily, and tried to pull down on Brawley, who blasted the fucker off his feet and dumped his dead ass back into the thick foliage lining the drive. The asshole's legs jutted skyward, his white Nikes painted crimson.

What a stupid way to die.

Brawley slid along the SUV, listening hard for a few seconds. Nothing. Just the hiss of the radiator's last bubbles and the siren growing louder with each passing second.

Correction, he thought. *Sirens.* Coming from multiple directions now.

He popped up, dropped back down, and gave himself a second to register what he'd glimpsed. Then he stood again just to make sure.

The inside of the SUV was a fucking slaughterhouse. Two men in there, both of them deader than hell.

The driver never made it out of his belt. It held him slumped to one side. The top half of his head was missing.

Another man lay stretched across the footwell of the second row, eyes staring up at the ceiling and already glazing over like those of a gutted deer. One of the man's legs was kicked over the other at a ridiculous angle like he was a showgirl in a chorus line. The cabin smelled like blood and shit and cordite.

Brawley went back around the SUV and took a chest harness off the man who'd been carrying the machine pistol.

Then he called for Nina, who was cursing as she unchained her moped and got it started. "Get on," she said, slapping the seat behind her. "Ohshitohfuckpissshitfuckfuck."

Brawley headed toward the bike then noticed movement at the edge of the drive. In his excitement, he'd forgotten the big bastard who'd come through the windshield, the same big bastard he'd warned not to come knocking just hours ago.

Gordo.

Brawley marched that way.

"What the hell are you doing?" Nina said. "We have to get out of here."

"Give me a second," he said and walked over to the asshole, who was pushing awkwardly up off the ground. "I told you what I'd do if you came knocking again," Brawley said, and blew a hole straight through the bastard's skull with his own pistol. Turning back toward Nina, he said, "I always keep my promises."

11

Senior Officer Jamaal Whittaker managed not to spill his coffee when Krupski slammed on the brakes, stopping inches behind the cruiser.

Or rather, one of the cruisers.

Three had already arrived. And more were coming. In fact, judging by the sirens, every cruiser, ambulance, and fire truck on the island was racing in this direction.

So Jamaal had to take care of this quickly.

Krupski leaned forward, scanning the scene with an enthusiastic expression.

Fucking rookies.

Cops were taping off the area and examining the particulars: a few dead people on the ground and a black SUV all shot to hell.

Without even checking the address, Jamaal knew this was the Mack girl's house. Shit. A pretty little pain in the ass, that one, her father's daughter to a tee.

Was she lying out there, riddled with bullets?

No. She was not.

Jamaal was certain of that much, at least. Beyond that,

however, he couldn't determine much. He couldn't even get a bead on the girl's direction, let alone her location.

That was strange.

Krupski whistled. "Wowzers, this is a proper mess, isn't it?"

Jamaal sipped his coffee. "If it isn't, it'll do the trick until a proper mess gets here."

This call was a true pain in the ass. Such shit timing.

Even if the call had only concerned an old lady worried about a cat halfway up a short tree it would've been a royal pain, given the timing.

Because as of thirty-four minutes ago, Jamaal had a *real* situation on his hands.

A situation?

No. An event was more like it. And he suspected that the event in question, which had kicked him straight in the medulla oblongata as he had been trying to nap at his desk, was going to develop into a major fucking shitstorm.

But duty called.

"Ready, Grandpa?" Krupski said, popping his door.

"You keep on with that Grandpa shit, you're buying me lunch again," Jamaal said, opening his door.

Jamaal scooted his bony ass to the edge of the seat, held his coffee close, and grabbed the top of the door. Then he hauled himself up, wincing as his hamstring locked and a line of fire burned across his ass and down his left leg, all the way to the sole of his foot.

Fucking sciatica.

"Back hurting you again?" Krupski asked.

"You're an observant son of a bitch," Jamaal growled. "You ought to be a cop or something."

Krupski laughed. Young and crisp and optimistic. Exactly the sort of pebble-brained rookie they needed to continue recruiting if they were going to keep this dog-and-pony

109

show rolling. Because if you didn't start out with stars in your eyes and an ass full of sunshine, there was no way on God's green Earth you could hang in until retirement.

Retirement. That was the word of the day. The word of the year. The word of the fucking century.

Retirement.

With just eight months, two weeks, three days, and a few hours left until Jamaal could start collecting his pension, the word retirement had become more than a word. It had become a song. A sweet song of promise. A fucking hymn.

Retirement. Dig it.

"Let's go, Grandpa," Krupski said with one of his big, good-natured, shit-eating grins. "Let's take care of this before the rest of the posse shows up."

"I warned you about that grandpa shit," Jamaal said, and started limping up the driveway toward the police officers, who would, of course, instantly recognize both men as federal agents.

Jamaal had never bothered to get more specific than feds. That notion got the job done fine, and he was too damned old to be worrying about artistry these days.

Past a certain age, you learned to pace yourself. He was the walking, talking personification of the 80/20 rule. Hell, anymore, he might even be 90/10.

Pick your battles, conventional wisdom advised, and in that case, at least, conventional wisdom was right.

Meanwhile, Jamaal had one hell of a battle unfolding before him. Not here. On the Latticework.

Actually, based on the waves of dread chilling him like a man coming down with the flu, Jamaal suspected that the clusterfuck presently unfolding on the Latticework might shape up to be not a battle but a full-blown war.

But rather than trying to get in front of that situation, he was here, sweeping the Mack girl's dust under the rug again.

He wondered distractedly if this mess had anything to do with the Mallory Square incident.

Yes, his gut chimed with certainty. It did have something to do with that. And so did the Mack girl.

Jamaal ground his teeth.

One of the Key West policemen approached, looking shaken.

Which was understandable, given the scene. At a glance, Jamaal perceived the basics. Five dead, one of them—that big-ass lump over at the edge of the drive—finished execution-style, a hollow-point to the back of the skull at point blank range.

Wowzers, as Krupski was irritatingly fond of saying.

The dead men were assholes. And a few of them were *known* assholes, he realized, their names rising unbidden into his mind like so many helium balloons drifting away from a toddler's birthday party.

Three of the dead men had been employees of Mr. Dutchman.

Of course, these cops didn't know shit about Mr. Dutchman, and five bullet-ridden corpses were five bullet-ridden corpses any way you cut it. So yeah, the cops were understandably shaken.

After all, these weren't the mean streets of South Chicago, where Jamaal had spent twenty-five grueling years on the beat and where he'd slipped on an icy sidewalk one winter, cracked his L-5, and conjured the cruel-ass demon named sciatica into his life. No, this was Key West, the posting Jamaal had been dreaming of since joining the force, and that meant that these conch cops didn't see even a murder per year. Now they were chalking lines around at several years' worth of homicides in a single driveway.

And no shooter yet identified, Jamaal realized.

The rattled cop, whose name tag read *Barclay*, nodded hello. "Thanks for coming."

"Wowzers," Krupski said. "That's a lot of dead people, Officer Barclay."

Barclay started talking about the scene, predictably compelled to surrender information to Jamaal, who nodded as Barclay's anxiety shifted gears, and his speech picked up speed, releasing a jumbled torrent of poorly organized details.

The number of bodies. Weapons and calibers. Three identities, all of them with outstanding warrants. The officers in attendance were thinking this was gang-related, maybe a drug deal gone bad, and Jamaal kept nodding, amused that even police officers, if their beat was tame enough, fell victim to overused Hollywood tropes.

"But the one thing we can't figure is the Escalade," Barclay said, nodding toward the shot-up vehicle. "The thing looks like it plowed straight into an oak tree, but here it sits in the middle of the driveway. And there's no way someone drove the thing here in that shape. Unless maybe someone brought it on a flatbed and dropped it off before the trouble started."

Jamaal scanned everything, letting Barclay ramble. Then Jamaal interrupted with an ingratiating smile and released a trickle of juice. "Relax, Officer Barclay. Everything's going to be okay."

Barclay exhaled a long breath, nodding, and Jamaal saw a good deal of tension leave the man's shoulders. Barclay had been hoping that everything would be all right. Helping someone to believe something was always easier than making them believe it.

Jamaal nudged Krupski and pointed to the nearest telephone pole.

Eager as always, Krupski didn't ask for clarification.

The cops shouted in dismay as the SUV whipped around,

pitching gravel into the air. Then the Escalade shot straight across the drive and crashed into the telephone pole. There was a loud crack. The upper half of the pole snapped away and smashed down on the SUV, crushing the hood, flattening the roof, and hauling wires through the surrounding foliage. One of the lines sheared away, hissing sparks like an electro-kinetic snake.

Shit. They couldn't ignore a downed power line. The last thing Jamaal needed was another stack of paperwork to complete later.

Meanwhile, Barclay and the boys in blue were losing their collective shit.

Jamaal almost spit out his coffee when he saw that one of them, a freckle-faced officer who looked about fifteen years old, had actually drawn his sidearm and was pointing it at the driver's side door of the demolished Cadillac.

Jamaal spread his arms. "It's okay, everyone. Everything is all right."

"The vehicle," Barclay stammered. "It just—"

"No," Jamaal interrupted, shaking his head and letting the juice flow. "You're all confused. The SUV hit that pole before you arrived. Remember?"

The cops exchanged looks, nodding. Someone laughed nervously.

"Everything is okay here," Jamaal assured them. "You have a pile of bodies to deal with, and that is unfortunate, but these men were scumbags. This is an open and shut case, obviously a drug deal gone bad."

The police officers mumbled in agreement.

Krupski went back to the car, pulled out a brick of heroine wrapped in a brown paper sack, and tossed it through the shattered back window of the Escalade.

Krupski was a pain in the ass with his lame jokes and nearly intolerable enthusiasm, but Jamaal liked that he didn't have to hold the rookie's hand during moments like this. Krupski was a go-getter and in that sense, at least, a perfect partner for a senior officer in the twilight years of his career.

The officers started asking what Krupski had tossed into the vehicle until Jamaal assured them that his partner hadn't done any such thing.

"All right," Jamaal said, "we'll get out of your hair now. It'll be like we weren't even here. Oh, one more thing. What happened here is completely unrelated to any of the residents, okay?"

The officers nodded.

"You've done your due diligence and can now report that you have located and interviewed the residents. They were not involved and were not harmed in any way. There is no need to follow up with them. They have no information."

Pointing at the home of the Mack girl, Jamaal said, "If anyone at the department seems curious about this resident, inform Officer Barclay, and he will call me."

Jamaal handed his card to Barclay, who promised to call if he heard anything.

"Thank you," Jamaal said. "Otherwise, you won't even remember that you have the card."

"Yes, sir."

An ambulance pulled into the driveway. Seconds later, a fire truck stopped alongside the road, lights flashing, making one hell of a racket.

"Okay, folks," Jamaal said, raising his voice and heading toward the car. "You're doing great work here. Thank you for your service. Could two of you please get these paramedics and firemen out of our way? Thank you."

Jamaal got back into the passenger seat. In the days of his youth, he had always insisted on driving. But he was too old for that shit now. And given everything presently sitting on his plate, if he climbed behind the wheel, he would probably get distracted, reenact Krupski's telekinetic handiwork, and plow straight into a damned phone pole.

Besides, the eager beaver liked to drive. Gave him something to do.

Krupski got in behind the wheel and shut his door, looking satisfied. "That went well."

"Let's get the hell out of here before I have to stop and talk to more people. I'm getting too old for this shit."

Krupski laughed and started pulling out but had to wait while the officers shooed the emergency personnel out of the way.

Jamaal was glad to be done here. He needed to head back to the office, lock himself away, and get busy figuring out what, exactly, had rocked the Latticework like a 9.5 magnitude earthquake.

If this call hadn't interrupted him so unfortunately, Jamaal might have already cracked the mystery.

Now, with so much time having passed and him having spent some of his juice rewiring the cops' memories, he would have a hard time catching up to the event. By this point, it might be lost to him altogether.

A maddening notion, that.

No matter how long he lived, Jamaal would never forget the moment the event had hit him. Something out there in the world had shifted sharply. Something huge and eventful, a game-changer of historic proportions. He'd been dozing pleasantly when the disturbance had smacked him right between the eyes like a sledgehammer.

The blast had left Jamaal reeling and he'd needed fifteen or twenty minutes just to regain his mental feet. Then, approximately two seconds after he'd shaken off the psychic hammer blow, this fucking call had come in and t-boned his intentions of unraveling the mystery.

Now, as they sat there waiting for these slowpokes to clear a path, Jamaal's frustration turned to anger.

That fucking Mack girl.

This wasn't the first time she had caused trouble. In fact, if Central had listened to Jamaal, none of this would've happened, because the Mack girl would still be locked up. And not in Fuggle County Correctional, either. He had suggested that they ship her ass straight to Gatlinburg and let the Chop Shop boys do their thing.

But Central had ignored his recommendation.

Jamaal didn't know what the Mack girl had gotten into here today, and he didn't much care. Okay, he was curious. Of course he was curious; it was his nature.

But the details of Nina Mack's ill-fated exploits could wait. At least until he'd had time to unravel more important things—like, you know, the biggest fucking psionic event to rock the Latticework since... shit... since the Culling last century.

As usual, the mere thought of the Culling turned his stomach. And as usual, he deflected further thoughts. If he started reminiscing about the role he'd been forced to play that dark night, it would only serve to ruin his appetite, his day, and his chances at solving the big mystery unfolding on the Latticework.

Trouble was, the Mack girl's bullshit, whatever it was, had left five fuggles dead on Jamaal's watch.

And the Order did not approve of dead fuggles. Let alone when psionic force had clearly played a part in those deaths.

Jamaal felt no pity for the dead men. The world was a better place without them. Besides, these asshats had died while running errands for the psi mafia, so they weren't exactly the innocent, ignorant fuggles the Order went to such extremes to shield from psionic harm.

Honestly, the situation had already worked itself out. There was no good reason to even report this to Central.

Or are you just justifying that notion because you want to buy more time to chase whatever the hell rocked the Latticework?

Perhaps. Perhaps.

But any Seeker in his shoes would do the same thing if they had even half a brain.

Meanwhile, the ambulance was finally pulling out, and Krupski was whistling a maddeningly cheerful tune, like a parrot who'd spent too much time in an elevator, memorizing muzak.

Jamaal pitched his perception out into the world again. There was still a chance to wrap up this case quickly and properly if he could only…

But no.

Somehow, the Mack girl had dropped completely off the radar. She wasn't dead; he'd know if she was dead. She had just gone dark. And that was strange. Beyond strange. Confounding.

Part of him, fueled by the inherent curiosity that came with being one of the top Seekers on the planet, latched onto the question of the Mack girl, and for an instant, he was tempted to pour everything into finding her.

Finding her and dealing with her.

But that would be foolishness, the sort of foolishness that kept Seekers from rising in the ranks or delayed their transfers to warmer climes or got them shit-canned when they had only eight and a half months until retirement.

Retirement.

A sweet, sweet psalm.

Jamaal couldn't let the Mack girl's disappearance serve as a further distraction, keeping him from the work he really needed to focus on.

The mysterious event had hit the Latticework hard

enough that even Australian Seekers must be scratching their heads and trying to sort it out.

Once he figured out what had rocked the Latticework, he would turn his attention back to this pain-in-the-ass interruption. He would track down the Mack girl and grill her hard. And then, if he had his way, they would ship her ass straight to the Chop Shop.

Unfortunately, he doubted that would happen. The Order had gotten softer and softer on unruly psi mages over recent years.

Recent years? he thought. *You mean recent* decades. *You're getting so old, you're remembering years as months.*

"Come the fuck on," Krupski said, and slapped the steering wheel. The firetruck had jackknifed across both lanes, immobilizing the ambulance that still blocked their exit. Krupski glanced at Jamaal. "What are you brooding about over there, partner?"

"Pater Janusian," Jamaal said truthfully. The Order had softened since Janusian's takeover in the wake of the Culling.

"Heavy subject," Krupski said. "Everything okay?"

"Everything's peachy keen," Jamaal said. On top of everything else, his hunger was kicking in now. At his age, he didn't eat very much, but when he was hungry, he was hungry, and using as much juice as he'd just released made him ravenous. He needed to eat before he even thought of trying to demystify the event. "I'm just thinking we wouldn't be sitting here with our thumbs up our asses if Janusian wasn't so soft."

"Soft?" Krupski laughed. "I wouldn't cross the man. Hell, I wouldn't even cross him for all the money you must have squirreled away in the bank."

"Janusian isn't soft on us," Jamaal said, "but he's soft on offenders. Back when I joined the force, if a psi mage fucked up, they paid for it."

"Oh boy. Here we go. And you used to walk to school through the snow every day, right? Uphill both ways?"

"Laugh away, son. I might be old, but I know what the fuck I'm talking about, and Central is too tolerant of psionic incontinence. Which makes our job much harder. You can only manipulate the truth so many times before even fuggles start detecting incongruencies. Janusian needs to crack down on rogue psi mages like the Mack girl, or he's going to jeopardize the entire community."

"Who's the Mack girl?" Krupski asked.

Oh hell, Jamaal thought. He really was getting old. He hadn't told Krupski about Nina Mack when they'd received the call. Why had he slipped up and mentioned her now? "Nothing," he said quickly, and released more of his precious juice. "She's nobody. In fact, I never mentioned her name."

Krupski blinked a couple times.

Jamaal realized during that brief interlude that he had blundered down a path he hadn't fully considered taking. So be it. He wouldn't report Mack. Not now. If he did, Central would tie him up chasing her instead of hunting down whatever was lighting up the Latticework.

And his curiosity was killing him.

He'd track down the Mack girl soon enough. And this time, he'd take care of her himself.

"Heh," Krupski said, returning to the conversation they'd been having before Jamaal had foolishly mentioned Mack. "You be sure and tell Pater Janusian that next time the big guy comes through for an inspection."

"Not going to happen," Jamaal said. "If Janusian even suspected that I was questioning his stances, he'd transfer me from Key West to Cleveland. Which is why..." He turned, laying a hand on his partner's shoulder. "We never had this conversation. We've been talking about lunch. You're in the mood for..."

Jamaal paused, deciding what he wanted.

"You're in the mood for tacos," Jamaal continued. "You want to go to Garbo's Grill." Then, grinning, he remembered and added, "And you're going to insist on picking up the tab."

He broke contact, and Krupski craned his neck, checking the rearview. "They finally cleared the drive. Hey, Grandpa, what do you say we hit Garbo's Grill? My treat."

"You sure?" Jamaal said.

"Hell yeah, I'm sure," Krupski said cheerily. "And don't give me shit about it. Wowzers, I'm hungry!"

They pulled onto the street and headed toward Caroline Street.

Jamaal reached out with his mind, checking the Lattice-work for any developments on the big disturbance. There was nothing new, but the entire network vibrated with activity. Seekers around the world had clearly registered the event and were now busy trying to root out the truth.

Which wouldn't have mattered to him so much if it weren't for one small detail that he feared they might also have detected, one teensy weensy factoid that might very well fuck up Jamaal's final months on the force.

Whatever had happened had happened here. Somewhere in the Florida Keys. Maybe even right here, in Key West.

Did the Seekers of the world suspect as much?

Stilling his mind and focusing on that question, Jamaal grafted his consciousness onto the Latticework for several seconds before retracting back into his own skull.

Yes, there were stirrings of such suspicions budding out along the Latticework.

Damn.

He bled blue like any worthwhile cop. He gave a shit. He really did. But he'd paid his dues. It had taken thirty-five years of hard work to earn a transfer to Key West. How cruelly ironic it would be if a powerful shitstorm slammed into his territory when he was only eight and a half months away from cutting permanent orders to Fort Living Room.

A second later, his intuition burst into mocking laughter.

Powerful? His gut implied. *Batten down the hatches, you old geezer. A Category 5 shitstorm is coming your way.*

12

Brawley sat on the U-shaped sofa in his RV, examining the firearms. Nina lay beside him, fighting sleep. She'd been struggling to stay awake ever since they reached the RV and lifted the moped inside.

That had been a bitch and a half. Her cute little scooter weighed three hundred pounds if it weighed an ounce.

But they couldn't afford to leave the thing out in the open for all the world to see. With a pile of corpses laying in Nina's driveway, Brawley had to assume that the cops were looking for her. And if they had talked to anyone who knew Nina, they were hunting her highly recognizable moped, too.

The strange thing about that, however, was what they were saying on TV. The 32" wall mount across from them was tuned to a local station, where special reports kept interrupting regular programming with breaking news updates that all seemed to say the same thing.

Authorities on the scene. Five dead. Two of the victims identified as having gang ties in Boca Raton.

Stuff Brawley would've expected.

Some of the other things they kept repeating, however, were a little surprising.

Authorities suspected a drug deal gone bad. None of the neighborhood's residents had been harmed or were being considered suspects.

Why would they say that? Was it the truth as far as the cops were concerned? Or was this some sort of trap to lull Nina into a false sense of security?

Brawley ejected the Smith & Wesson's magazine and racked the slide, clearing the chamber. Setting the pistol on the dinette table, he thumbed rounds out of the magazine, counting them up on the table before him. Seven. Eight, counting the hollow-point at his feet.

"Holy shit," Nina said drowsily. "I can't believe that actually happened."

The shootout had rattled her cage pretty hard.

Brawley, on the other hand, felt strangely calm. He'd always figured if he ended up killing somebody, it would weigh on him. Not so much. Not at all, in fact. They had tried to kill his woman, and he had responded logically, decisively, and without mercy.

Now those assholes were dead. End of story. No sense feeling bad about it.

Not that Nina was expressing remorse. She was just worried about the ramifications. And that made sense, even if he didn't share her anxieties.

Part of that was this psionic bullshit that had overtaken him. He felt strong. Strong and sharp and ready to roll. Dominant as fuck, if he was honest about it.

But part of his calm was just Brawley being Brawley. You spend your life climbing onto the world's rankest bulls, ignoring broken bones and torn ligaments, you didn't startle easy.

At the same time, he knew this was a real problem. So while he wasn't worried, he was serious.

"Well, you'd better believe it, darlin," he said, "because it did happen. We can't afford to pretend it didn't."

He picked up the last cartridge, wiped it clean, and fed it back into the magazine. Then he replaced the magazine, set the Smith & Wesson on the cushion beside him, and turned his attention to the machine pistol.

The Mac-10 was a stubby little thing, ten or eleven inches of stamped metal fitted with a folding stock and a box mag that held thirty rounds of .45 ammunition. Firing full auto with a short barrel like that, he'd be lucky to hit the broadside of a barn at fifty yards. It sure wouldn't be much good for hunting antelope out on the floodplains, where Brawley bagged animals all the way out to nine hundred yards.

What the machine pistol was good for, as he had proven in Nina's driveway, was rapidly blowing holes through assholes at close range. So even though getting caught with a weapon like this meant a felony charge, Brawley decided to hold onto the thing until their present troubles had concluded. He had a feeling he wasn't done killing assholes, at close range or otherwise.

Why didn't these stupid sons of bitches have a suppressor on this thing? It would've cut down on the racket, increased the barrel length, and doubled as a foregrip, stabilizing the weapon, especially on full auto. The barrel was already threaded, so the mod wouldn't even require a gunsmith.

Must be Nina's would-be hitman hadn't planned on firing the thing. Not really. Not even if firing the thing had been the sole purpose of the job and the machine pistol itself. Some part of the man's mind must have still been play-acting, valuing the menace of a mean-looking subcompact over the utility of a quieter, more deadly tool.

Hell, if the man had been serious, he would've carried a Mossberg instead of a machine gun.

What an idiot.

The chest rig Brawley had hauled off the dead man featured six pouches, three on three, the back row filled with box mags for the machine pistol, the front row stuffed with magazines full of 10mm ammo, which was useless to him now.

He pulled the 10mm magazines and set them aside. Then he swapped the machine pistol's empty box mag for a full one.

He wished he had a shotgun and one of his hunting rifles, the .308 or even his old model 94 .32 special lever-action Winchester, a cowboy rifle if ever there was one. But they were all back on the ranch. He hadn't come here to hunt.

What he did have was his carry piece, a well-worn, light-weight XDS .45 that fit his big hands perfectly, along with its equally well-worn leather holster, which now sat comfortably inside his waistband, the feel of it against his body as familiar as the caress of a lover.

Again, he was tempted to ditch the 9mm, but he only had the chest rig rounds and a single box of ammo for his XDS, so he figured he might as well hold onto the Smith & Wesson at least until they got out of town.

"What do we do now?" Nina asked.

"I reckon we should hold off on seeing your brother and dad and hole up until Sage gets off work."

"Guess we'd better wear disguises."

"Something like that. I can put on a hat," he said, thinking, *but not my cowboy hat, not until I ride again*.

"I'd change my clothes, but they're all back at my apartment."

"We'll get you clothes. And a hat. Not too many drop-dead gorgeous women walking around with purple hair.

Then we'll see Sage's super Seeker and get the hell out of town."

"Okay," Nina said, and Brawley knew she was fighting hard against sleep. Then she roused and stared up at him, her mismatched eyes full of emotion. "I was so worried about you back there, babe."

"Don't you worry about me," he said, and gave her a kiss. "I'm hard to kill. Go on and get some sleep now."

He didn't have to tell her twice. Five seconds later, Nina was out.

She had been amazed by the power that she had generated, smashing the SUV, but the expenditure had staggered her, leaving her too weak to keep fighting. That's why she'd staggered through the fence gate rather than staying to help him.

Apparently, once psi mages burned the gas in their tank, the only way to refuel was rest.

Did the same rules apply to Brawley if he was a so-called power mage?

He had no idea. It was one of many questions he had for his girls.

What a crazy twenty-four hours. Shit, not even. More like eighteen or twenty hours.

Whatever the case, in less than a day, he'd banged two beautiful women, fallen in love with both of them, killed five assholes, and oh yeah, discovered that he had some kind of magical power.

Not magical, he corrected himself. *Psionic.*

Sage had explained that while magical power came from external sources, psionic power came from within.

Whatever.

If it looked like magic and smelled like magic...

Speaking of psionics, he needed to practice. And that sounded good, appealing to both his train-till-you-bleed-

and-then-train-some-more nature and the overwhelming curiosity he'd felt since making it with Sage.

He pushed the machine pistol across the table, pulled off his boots, and got comfortable on the couch.

Nina was snoring softly.

Man, was she a good-looking woman. And cool. And super fucking powerful.

He was sorry that her life had gotten turned upside down, but he wouldn't change that, not if changing it meant him never meeting her in the first place.

He loved Nina and didn't give a tin shit whether that made sense or not.

He closed his eyes and tried to locate the power in his mind.

A second later, there it was, glowing brightly within the darkened cave he'd visited earlier. The strand was glowing much more brightly now than it had at breakfast.

All right. Now to draw the power.

Honestly, he had no idea what to do. But that wasn't going to stop him. The best way to learn something was usually to jump on and take a ride.

He could feel the power's heat and motion. It was hotter and stronger than before. As he concentrated, something shifted, and he once again had a sense of his will as an entity unto itself, a force within the cavernous non-space of his mind.

He focused on the invisible flame, and something interesting happened.

He could see the strands. Not with his eyes, of course, but with some kind of mental eye that had not previously been available to him.

Had opening his Seeker strand made that inner eye available to him?

Perhaps. He reckoned probably so.

The strands wavered, a distant blur of faint illumination in the shadowy reaches of his mind.

He drove his consciousness forward through the void, and the strands grew warmer and brighter and stronger. More distinct.

There were two clumps of wavering strands, one red, one yellow, swaying back and forth among several grayish hummocks, out of which stretched a thicket of ash-colored strands as stiff and motionless as petrified trees. These gray clumps—he counted five—gave off no heat.

Seven orders. Seven strands.

The gray strands must be his five untapped power sources.

Brawley's curiosity spiked. He pushed forward for a closer look.

The red and yellow strands brightened, growing warmer, and he felt a new sensation, something like urgency emanating from the colors.

But he focused on the lifeless, gray strands. Choosing one clump at random, he reached out, trying to coax it toward him.

There was no response.

One by one, he tested the gray tangles, and one by one, they remained lifeless. No heat, no motion. Nothing.

So be it.

He reached out, beckoning to the luminescent fibers, and his mind exploded in a blinding, burning rush of heat and light.

Brawley recoiled instinctively and came to on the couch. The mind-space and strands were gone.

Nina stirred, mumbling softly.

He stroked her head gently, his fingertips whisking over her stubbled temple and combing through the long, purple tresses.

Nina settled back into her slumber.

What, exactly, had happened in there?

He'd coaxed the strands, and they'd both pounced on him like dogs welcoming their master. Trouble was, these dogs weighed a ton each and burned at about four hundred degrees.

All right, then. He'd need to fit a valve onto his coaxing. Gain a little precision here. And he couldn't have both of them hitting him at once.

According to Nina, the idea with psionics was locate the power, draw it together, shape it, and use it. You could learn different actions over time, some more intuitive than others. Each of these had a certain cost attached.

But he was getting ahead of himself.

He went back in. A second later, he was right back where he'd been. The colorful strands had retracted back into their clumps. They pulsed brightly, throbbing with eagerness. He couldn't help but think of whining hounds aching to come off the lead.

He concentrated on his will, shaping it once more into a grasping appendage, and reached out toward the clump of red strands.

Strands of both colors rushed toward him like striking snakes.

Easy, Brawley thought. *Easy there.*

He held out the hand of his consciousness, allowing the strands to bump against it.

That's it. Easy now. You're okay. He kept his thoughts as calm and soothing as the voice he used to gentle a half-broken mare.

He took his time, experimenting with different tones, opening and closing his mind's hand, and permitting just a whisper of invitation.

Finally, he managed to separate one of the red strands

from the tangled red-and-yellow mass. Once more, he was reminded of having latched onto an overloaded power cable. Only this time, the heat and vibration were even stronger.

Again and again, he attempted to haul back on the strand. Again and again, he met with failure.

Then, remembering Nina saying that he couldn't force it, he concentrated on the single strand and rather than trying to pull it toward him, called to it softly in a mental whisper.

It worked.

The strand pushed toward him. All of the strands did, but mostly the red one he held in his mind's hand.

He hauled back experimentally, and the strand came to him, dragging behind it more power. It was heavy, like drawing a full bucket out of a deep well.

With each pull, the red power he'd already gathered coiled in an ever-increasing pile that grew warmer and vibrated more powerfully. Slowly, the red fibers untangled themselves from the yellow and drifted forward, and he was able to gather them as well.

Soon, he was able to grasp all of them at once. He tugged, and a wave of power rose from the blackness within his mind.

A short time later, his consciousness—which increasingly felt like not just a hand but an entire figure, a thing approaching some shadowy representation of his corporeal self—reeled, surrounded by a swirling mass of hot, red energy that coiled thickly around him, spinning up and up and up into the dark reaches of his mind.

It was awesome. Power beyond power.

And at the moment, totally useless.

He needed to draw it in more tightly if he was going to stand a chance at shaping the stuff. With his mind's hands, he started scooping away sections of the luminescence and cramming it down at his feet. And yes, his consciousness had feet now, or something like feet, anyway, and they stood upon a dark pediment of sorts. Soon he was using the feet of his consciousness to tamp the bright red stuff down like so much dirt and gravel.

Haul, tamp. Haul, tamp. He fell into a rhythm. Gathering more and more of the stuff with each pull and packing it down into a mass that fairly sizzled with heat and pent-up force.

Finally, he figured enough was enough.

Most of the red stuff was still pillaring up around him like a tornado of lava, but he decided to draw no more.

The tamped mass upon which his inner self now stood was already seething and humming with power, and honestly, he didn't know whether he was standing on a fire-cracker or fourteen tons of C-4.

He had no clue what to do next. In fact, he really didn't know what he'd managed to do beyond the fact that he had managed to do something.

Had all of that amounted to simply gathering energy? Or had his mental tamping been the shaping that Nina had mentioned?

If so, had he shaped it correctly?

Hell, he didn't know. But he sure was curious.

Not curious enough, however, to go off half-cocked and blow his damn fool head off.

For a second, he paused there, examining the scene and looking for a way to separate the tamped energy from the swirling storm of force. But he could see no way to do that, no way to parcel up one bundle from the main mass.

Was this normal?

How could he—

Oh, to hell with it, he thought, and then he was back in himself, back in his real-world, walking, talking body, laughing now because the whole thing was cool and crazy and totally fucking absurd, and because here he was, some kind of mental magician stockpiling power, still struggling against his natural tendency to keep fighting, keep pushing, to keep climbing back on the damn bull no matter how much it hurt or the likelihood of getting stomped or gored or maybe even killed.

Yes, he wanted to go back in. Yes, he wanted to try to use his powers. But all his years of training and riding had also taught him that sometimes, climbing back onto the bull was a damned fool idea. And right now, lighting the fuse of the red bomb pulsing in his mind would probably turn out to be the damned foolest of all damned fool ideas.

He sat there grinning for a while, thinking, wishing Nina would wake up but knowing she needed her rest.

He didn't know what to do with himself.

Finally, he decided to keep it simple. He got up and went to the pantry and pulled his medicine ball from the lower cubby then grabbed one of the dozen boxes of Fruit Loops he kept on board.

Five minutes later, he was standing on the medicine ball, working his balance while he ate a bowl of cereal and watched the latest news report. The police chief, a rugged looking guy in his forties, stood at a podium surrounded by microphones, doing damage control.

"This is an unprecedented event in Key West," the chief told reporters. "We will, of course, continue to investigate, but this really appears to be an open and shut case. None of the men involved were Key West residents, and we have no reason to believe that the organizations they represented are not otherwise active in our city. Judging on forensic evidence, eyewitness accounts, and security camera footage, we do not at this time believe any additional persons were involved in this event."

Strange, Brawley thought. *A strange thing to think, even, let alone report.*

The police chief paused, and a wave of jumbled questions washed over him.

"The main thing I want to get across," the police chief said, "is that Key West remains the safe, friendly town it always has been. This was an unfortunate but isolated event, and it is behind us now. Residents and tourists alike are encouraged go on about business as usual. Relax and have your fun. There is no threat, and as always, the Key West Police Department will be out there helping to keep you safe."

13

Later, Brawley left Nina a note and headed out to pick up some stuff. He had a couple of hours to kill before meeting Sage and figured he might as well grab things while Nina rested.

Besides, he was dying of hunger. Man could not live on Fruit Loops alone.

This part of town felt less like Key West and more like Anytown, Florida. Other than Publix, he saw a pawn shop, a liquor store, a Subway, a consignment shop, and a movie theater that was either shut down or in bad need of a facelift.

Colorful graffiti decorated the large dumpster and row of garbage trucks parked in front of the dilapidated theater. One patch of straightforward green ink read *Keep Key West Weird*. As Brawley read the words, they blurred, revealing psi graffiti underneath the paint: *We're trying, asshole*.

Further down the line, he saw more restaurants, more shops, and a few big department stores.

He kept a pretty good roll of cash onboard the RV, but with everything that was going on, he hit the ATM and pulled out an additional three hundred bucks.

It was still strange, even after all these months, having money. You grow up poor, you never quite believe that you're flush with cash no matter what your bank statements say.

At Subway, he wolfed down a foot-long cold cut combo. Then he went into the consignment shop next door, where he picked up a turquoise hoodie and yellow sweatpants for Nina, along with a ball cap the color of a bluebonnet in April.

He would have grabbed her some shoes, too, but he had no idea what size she wore. Besides, if there was one area in his experience where women were extremely particular it was in the realm of footwear.

Girls and their shoes. Coming between them was like doing the jitterbug between a mama bear and her cubs. Ill-advised, men of the world, ill-advised.

Much safer to hand Nina the disguise and some cash, point the way to Champs and TJ Maxx, and tell her to have at it.

At the liquor store, he grabbed three cases of Bud and enough liquor to kill a bull, blowing through a good portion of the money he'd pulled from the ATM. The rest of the cart he filled with chips, pretzels, and cheese curls because most of the hot women he'd known lived primarily on junk food.

Nina was still sleeping.

Brawley stowed the stuff and left again. In Publix, he stocked up on the essentials: SpaghettiOs, beef jerky, milk for his Fruit Loops, and a few rolls of Copenhagen.

He hadn't slept in a long time, and he'd sure been through the ringer, but he felt good. Great, in fact. His old injuries still pained him, but what the hell? He'd been carrying those pains around for so long he'd almost miss them if they left now.

Well, not really. But their absence would certainly be peculiar.

Meanwhile, he felt energized and strong. And if he concentrated, he could feel the energy he'd drawn up sitting in his mind, humming away like a whole-house generator waiting for a storm.

His curiosity remained cranked to the max, too. His thoughts shifted now to the questions Sage's friend Hazel might answer.

What was Brawley's real name, his true name?

Who had his birth parents been? Why had they given him up for adoption? And why had they cloaked his aura?

What did it mean, being a power mage? He understood that it meant having the potential to tap all seven strands, but what else? The girls had been awed by the idea, both amazed and frightened.

Just how powerful could he become, anyway? And what would that mean? He had a general sense of what psi mages could do, but that was it.

Just how hard was it going to be to hide this shit from the Order? Although Brawley missed riding bulls, he had also been looking forward to a quiet life on the ranch far from the packed stadiums, booming speakers, and blasting pyrotechnics of the PBR events. The last thing he wanted now was a life on the run.

No sooner had he considered this thought than an icy wave of dread washed over him.

Had that frigid pang been some Seeker shit, a bad omen dropping a mystical ice cube down the back of his shirt?

Nothing he could do about it now, one way or the other.

When he got back to the RV, Nina was up. She was bright-eyed and ready to roll.

Brawley popped a can of SpaghettiOs with meatballs and asked her if she wanted any. She said no, so he stood there eating them out of the can like a true Winnebago warrior.

Nina came over and asked for a bite. He handed her the spoon, and five minutes later, his SpaghettiOs were gone.

"Thanks," she laughed. "Guess I was hungrier than I thought."

Curious creatures, women.

Brawley filled her in about the news reports, but he still didn't want her running around town, so they agreed to split up. He would pick up Sage at five then go with her to meet Hazel. Nina would put on the hat and sweats, hit the department stores, and take it easy in the RV.

"I stand corrected," Nina said, scanning the vehicle. "I had no idea that RVs were so cool."

He gave her the grand tour. She asked about his hat, which sat gathering dust on the top shelf of the pantry, but he realized that he didn't feel like explaining his reasons for leaving it in there.

Someday, he'd climb up on a bull again. Then and only then would he put that hat back on his head. And that was nobody's business but his.

"You need any cash, this is where I keep it," he said, pulling out the can of dehydrated potatoes. He tilted the can, shifting the flakes to reveal a stash of plastic baggies filled with tens and twenties, several thousand dollars in all.

Nina's eyes got huge. "How do you know I won't drive off with everything?"

"Never happen," he said. "You're crazy about me."

They laughed and kissed, and that turned into more. After they made love, they showered together, which proved to be pleasantly awkward in the little stall. So much so, in fact, that they ended up doing it again.

One thing was for sure. Becoming a power mage had strapped a jet pack to his stamina.

Brawley left Nina the keys, the cash, and the machine pistol, happy to see that she knew her way around firearms.

Then he kissed her goodbye and went to see his other woman.

————

Sage was waiting for him on the steps of the library.

For just a second, Brawley thought their reunion might be awkward. At least with Nina, they'd had time to talk and grab drinks before getting freaky. With Sage, on the other hand…

But the beautiful librarian came straight into his arms and kissed him deeply. Sage was different than Nina. Taller and less curvy. Her kissing wasn't feverish and desperate like Nina's, but her kisses were soft and deliberate, full of subtle passion and joy.

When they stepped apart, Sage's eyes were gleaming. "I enjoy being intimate with you, my power mage." She sounded almost sultry, and he detected half a grin, which he found disproportionately endearing.

"I enjoy being intimate with you, too," he said. "Which way to your friend's place?"

She nodded down the street, and they started walking. "Tell me what happened at Nina's."

"You sensed that?"

"Not initially," Sage said. "Everyone at work was buzzing about it. Then yes, I did spend a good deal of time checking in on you today."

"How could you? I thought we were cloaked."

"You are," she said, "but I put a psi sensor on your belt buckle and Nina's nose ring."

"You LoJacked my belt buckle?"

"Essentially. But a psi sensor allows me to occasionally observe the sensor's surroundings, so it would be more appropriate to say I bugged your buckle."

"That's creepy."

"Not at all," Sage said. "We are bound and thus have no secrets between us. Besides, I am happy that I did. It allowed me to check on you after the news story broke. And…" She broke off, and her pale cheeks pinkened.

"What?"

"I tuned in while the two of you were being intimate."

Brawley laughed. "Like I said, creepy."

"I could hear you and see you and even smell the sex. I became so aroused that I masturbated through multiple orgasms."

Brawley had to grin at her weird phrasing, but imagining this beautiful blonde swept into a rapture of voyeuristic masturbation in the back room of the library, he felt himself going hard again.

"It's really quite interesting," Sage said.

"You can say that again."

"These urges and emotions are very much out of character for me," Sage explained, slipping her hand into his, "but ever since we bound our energies, I can't stop thinking about you and Nina. I have never been in love before. Or lust. And now I find myself immersed in both conditions." She frowned thoughtfully. "I am concerned, actually, that our passions might distract me from my work."

"Well, darlin, there are worse fates than fucking too much. After we get back from seeing your mentor, we can scratch that itch for you."

She gave his hand a squeeze. "I would like that very much, Master."

"Master?" Brawley laughed.

"You are a power mage," Sage explained. "*My* power mage. You bound me. When a power mage binds a psi mage, his energy both empowers and dominates hers. You strengthened me, and I'm very curious to see what all of this power can do.

"But you also broke me. I am yours. Completely yours. It is the natural relationship of a devotee to her power mage. Nina and I only wish to serve and please you... Master."

"Well, that's nice to hear," Brawley said, "and for my part, I feel very attracted to you. And very protective. Hell, I don't even know you yet, but I already love you. Makes no sense, but there you have it."

Now Sage was beaming. "It does make sense, Master! In fact, this is an extremely well-documented phenomenon. When a power mage binds a psi mage, their affections are both instantaneous and eternal. Our psionic bonding joined our deepest selves without the clumsy fumbling of traditional courting or the parceling together of some societal and emotional contract. As soon as our energies intertwined, I loved you, and I will love you until I die. Those emotions will only grow from this moment, as will your dominance and my submission."

Brawley considered that for a moment. She was right. He could feel that in his bones and also in his blood, his heart, and every fiber of his being. But one thing still felt wrong. "Good to know, darlin, but how about you stop calling me Master, okay? That feels a little weird."

"Okay," Sage said, pinkening again. They were silent for several steps, then she said, "May I still call you Master when we are being intimate?"

"Whatever turns you on."

"You turn me on. Your power and the power you give me. I was born with a high psi score, and I've worked hard to perfect my technique, thereby maximizing the effectiveness of Seeker skills and reducing the energy expenditure required by each psionic action. But I'm not boiling over with potential like Nina and you.

"When you and I bound our energy, we boosted Nina all the way to 157, which means there are fewer than two hundred psi mages in the entire country more powerful than she."

"Wow."

"Yes. I can't help but envy her power, even though envy is an absurd abomination in light of the Truth. But power like Nina's would be such an advantage in unraveling the mysteries of the universe. That is what I do, day after day. I squeeze every bit of juice from each point at my disposal, ceaselessly chasing the great mystery."

"Don't you get tired of it?"

She laughed, sounding incredulous. "Not at all. In fact, I curse sleep because it robs me of time I might otherwise use to delve more deeply into truth."

"Sounds like I've hitched my wagon to a bona fide nerdy girl."

That made her smile. "The nerdiest. And I couldn't be happier. You've given me so much power, which is wonderful, but you are wonderful, too, a mystery unto yourself. As is Nina. I am excited to explore both of you. And your penis is unusually large, adding to my physical pleasure."

Brawley laughed.

"Why do you laugh?" Sage asked. At this point, he couldn't tell whether she was serious or yanking his chain.

"Nothing," he said. "You're just going to take some getting used to is all."

"Did I say something wrong? If so, I apologize. I know that my social skills have suffered over the years, but—"

He silenced her with a kiss, which the blond beauty returned eagerly.

"Darlin, you didn't say anything wrong. I'm glad you're happy. I'm happy, too. You're interesting and beautiful. I'm tickled that you're my woman."

"I enjoy your colloquialisms," she said. "I am also 'tickled' to be your woman. It is exciting. Of course, you are a power mage, so I am literally bound to adore and obey you, but many power mages down through history were cruel and made their psi-spouses incredibly unhappy."

A disturbing question drifted across his sunny thoughts. "This power mage thing, it's not going to change me, is it?"

"Of course it will change you."

"I'm not talking about opening strands and doing psionic shit. I mean, am I still going to be me? This shit isn't going to turn me mean or something, is it?"

She looked thoughtful for a second, staring at him as they walked. "There is much darkness in you, psi-husband. Darkness that will grow in step with your power. Your future lies at the edge of oblivion. The only light I see is fire. The only sounds I hear are the crackling of flames, the screaming of your enemies, and the soft patter of blood raining down."

Brawley said nothing, taking a second to let her twisted prophecy settle in.

"You will kill many people," Sage said, "but you will not mistreat me. Nor will you mistreat Nina."

He relaxed a little. "That's good to know."

"As to your future psi-wives," Sage said, "I cannot yet say. There are too many variables at play, not the least of them being your cloak, which interrupts your connection to the Latticework. And of all the variables in the universe, love remains one of the least predictable. The whims of the heart are most unsatisfyingly quantum in nature."

"Yeah, you are definitely going to take some getting used to," Brawley said. He didn't understand everything that Sage said, and it was all strange to him, but his curiosity was burning brighter than ever. "As to those future psi-wives, we'll just see. I'd like a chance to get to know my first two before I even think about adding others."

"Understandable," Sage said. "But you must add others. You are a power mage. You need to locate five additional women to open your remaining strands and teach you the ways of their orders. Aren't you excited?" Her voice thickened with awe. "I would be so curious to experience everything."

"I am curious," he said. "But apparently, once I bond with a woman, it's forever. And not just for me. For her, too. And for you and Nina. That's asking a lot from all of you."

"Yes," she said, "but you will also be rewarding us. Each time you bond with a new woman and open another strand, your existing wives will experience a permanent boost in power. If the pattern holds true, you will boost our psi score around 2% each time you take a psi-wife. Once you open your seventh strand,"—she paused for a second, blinking rapidly—"Nina will have a psi score of 173, making her one of the most powerful psi mages in the nation. My own score will be 158, making me more powerful than all but around twenty Seekers across the nation. That might be enough…." She trailed off, sounding awed again.

"Enough for what?"

"To know the Truth, of course. Oh, it would take many years and much work, but I am undaunted by the challenge. There are different schools of thought within our order, but I believe that with the proper skills, requisite time, and sufficient power, a Seeker could grasp the ultimate, all-encompassing Truth. My life's goal is to understand the Latticework in its entirety, all at once.

"I want to know all things, past and present, simultaneously, and to grasp their interrelation with such perfection that I will be able to extrapolate all things to the end of time, predicting anything and everything with absolute precision and certainty, solving the mysteries of the universe—time, space, existence, everything—and using these answers to solve the great question upon which all unknown matters are but facets: the Truth. Every problem solved, every question answered, every possibility chased out to its conclusion, all of it at once, everything relative to everything else, none of it meaningful without the whole."

"That's quite a goal," Brawley said.

"Yes," Sage said. "It is the butterfly effect writ large, a goal hinged upon the notion that at its base, the universe is orderly." She laughed. Bitterly, it seemed to Brawley. "But I am also engaged in a philosophical conundrum, because knowing all things would, ironically, mean knowing only one thing, the Truth; and to know one thing without relevance to other things is to know nothing. Beholding the Great Truth would simultaneously sate and destroy my curiosity. There would be nothing left to discover. Even my discovery itself would be part of the whole. There would be no celebration, for my own consciousness would likewise disappear into the Great Truth."

Brawley whistled. "That's the heaviest shit I ever heard. You might want to pump the brakes before you get to the end."

Sage laughed. "I do like you, psi-husband. Very much. And speaking of pumping brakes, I am looking forward to traveling in your RV."

"Wait, how did you—" but Brawley didn't bother to finish. How did she know about his RV? She was a Seeker. They just knew shit. He didn't understand how it all worked, but he was looking forward to learning to use his yellow energy. That would be sweet. Unless, of course, he had visions of impending doom. If he did, would those truths be set in stone, or would he have a shot at altering his would-be future?

"I grew up in an RV," Sage said. "My parents were both Seekers, and they wanted to see and experience everything.

They homeschooled me, and we traveled all over the Western Hemisphere."

"That must've been something. I barely made it off the ranch as a kid."

Sage nodded. "We saw a lot and learned a lot. Since I have an eidetic memory, I remember all of it."

"Does that mean you remember everything?"

"It does. You will, too, soon enough. It's one of the first things you will learn as a Seeker. Memory, analysis, danger sense, detecting falsehoods, reading auras, touching the Latticework. These are the fundamentals of our Order. But until my strand opened at sixteen, I really didn't care about any of this. My parents were dedicated to seeking the truth, so I was terribly lonely as we drove from place to place.

"I wanted to be around other kids. I wanted to try school. And because I did not at that point have an eidetic memory or abilities like my parents, I felt stupid. Most frustrating of all, however, was my inability to glimpse the future. No child likes to be controlled 24/7 by her parents. But it is maddening when you are locked in an RV with two Seekers. They would say, 'Don't do that, Sage, or this will happen.' And it drove me crazy, not only because I was a kid, trying to find my way in the world, but also because they were right. Every. Single. Time. It was *father knows best* and *mother knows best* rolled together and multiplied by infinity. And meanwhile, I just wanted to have some random fun."

As a man who had always valued his independence above almost everything else, Brawley reeled back from that notion like a horse from a brushfire. "That must've been torture."

"It was," Sage said. "Then, one morning shortly after my sixteenth birthday, I woke before first light. I felt strange. Very awake and very curious. My parents were still sleeping. Moving quietly, I slipped from the RV.

"We were parked in the desert. Dawn was breaking to the

east, just beyond the mountains, bronzing their purple peaks with the first light of day. Everything was so vibrant. The sights, the sounds, the smells. I crouched there in my thin nightgown and scooped up a handful of grit and let it sift away between my fingers, counting the individual grains with an effortless speed and accuracy like nothing I had ever experienced before that moment. And suddenly, discovering the exact number of grains in that handful seemed to me the most important thing in the world."

"How many were there?"

"Seven thousand eight hundred and twelve," she said without hesitation. "More than the number of stars we can see with the naked eye. But no sooner had I completed my calculation than I was gripped with new compulsions. I set off, counting my steps as I trekked across the desert toward the nearest ridge, which I scaled.

"Near the top, I discovered a cave. A part of me had known it would be there, I realize now. And inside the cave, I found this." She extended her wrist, drawing his attention to a simple leather bracelet and an understated pendant of rough-cut gray stone.

"What is it?"

"Petrified wood," Sage said. "The remains of a gingko tree that first broke from its seed 212 million years ago. In 1786, a seven-year-old Navajo child named Chooli discovered the petrified tree and carried this piece into the cave, where she hid it from her brother. She visited the cave three times but eventually forgot all about the petrified wood as other prizes seized her imagination.

"If you like, I could tell you all about Chooli's life, as well as the life of her family members, and their ancestors. I could give you the names, addresses, and phone numbers of her living descendants, though none of them have ever heard of

Chooli, who was frankly not a significant person, historically speaking.

"Except to me." Sage rolled the pendant between her thumb and forefinger. "Because when I first examined this petrified wood, I knew nothing. I thought it was stone. But I was consumed by curiosity. I knew nothing about it or the cave or Chooli. I only knew that I needed to know. It took months of intense study beneath the instruction of my parents for me to unravel the mysteries of the petrified gingko."

"That's how it all started, huh?" Brawley said.

"The old me died that day in the desert. I used to be such a fool. A pretty little fool wracked by loneliness. I could have been seeking the Truth, but I just wanted to have fun."

"There are worse sins," Brawley said.

"Yes, I know that now," she said, and gave his hand a squeeze. "Especially since meeting you. In fact, having spent much of my day pining for you, I can't help but feel a little sad to remember the hopeful, desperate girl I used to be. I even feel sorry for her."

"You're still her."

"No. She is gone."

"Bullshit. You're still her. And you're also still Sage the super nerd."

She laughed. "That is a remarkably Seeker-ish thing to say, husband. I just don't feel like her anymore. Which is sad, I suppose, because she would have loved you."

"Correction," Brawley said, pulling her into him. "She does love me. And so do you."

"I won't deny it, husband," Sage said. Then she squeezed his hand and pointed to a strip of small shops. "We have arrived. Prepare to meet the most powerful Seeker in the Florida Keys."

14

T he Third Eye, the colorful yet faded sign read. *Curios sold. Fortunes Told.*

An addendum in less faded script announced, *Walk-ins Welcome.*

A second later, another addendum appeared, this one bleeding through the main sign in blocky psi script: *PSI MAGE DISCOUNTS.*

The Third Eye was a long, narrow shop lit only by the diffuse sunlight falling through the smudged plate glass. Near the door, four battered chairs were pulled into a rough circle around a steamer trunk, atop which a short pedestal held a murky crystal sphere the size of a bowling ball.

The rest of the shop was a dusty firetrap packed with knickknacks and bric-a-brac, no rhyme or reason to any of it beyond a layer of united dust.

An ancient woman emerged from a side room, walking with a cane.

A loose and colorful gown of tie-dyed silk draped her emaciated frame, and her considerable shock of frizzy white hair was pulled back in a haphazard ponytail, making her look like an ancient hippie, an affect exacerbated by the large peace sign pendant dangling on a silver chain from her scrawny neck. Hazel's hands were gnarled with arthritis, and behind the thick lenses of her wire-rim glasses, her rheumy eyes were, in fact, brownish-green in color, making Brawley wonder if her name was a coincidence or if a Seeker parent had foreseen her eye color and named her accordingly.

"Hello Hazel," Sage said.

Hazel blinked several times, looking back and forth between them. "Hello Sage," she said, and her rheumy gaze paused on Brawley, looking him up and down. "And hello to you, young man. I knew you were coming today. Both of you."

"Nice to meet you, ma'am, I'm—"

"No," Hazel interrupted. "Don't tell me your name. That is for later. That's why you're here, isn't it, Sage, to uncover his true name?"

"Partly," Sage said.

"And you're in love," Hazel laughed.

Sage blushed again. She looked very cute, and Brawley felt another surge of affection. "I am."

"With him, I suppose?"

"Yes. With him… and with another."

"And another?" Hazel chuckled. "What interesting lives you young people lead." Then the old woman's eyes narrowed. "Sage, you've changed. You've become more powerful. Far more powerful, in fact."

"Yes," Sage said, "but please do not delve into my development yet, Hazel."

The old woman blew a raspberry. "Secrets. Speaking of which, I have thus far honored the cloak you placed around your friend here. Shall I continue to do so or may I peek behind the curtain?"

"You may examine him shortly," Sage said, "but first, I would prefer to explain a few things."

Hazel frowned. To Brawley, she said, "Speech is so tiresome when you're my age. So slow and fraught with misinformation."

The old Seeker sighed and said to Sage, "I will endure your explanations, dear, but first humor an old woman and give her the chance to rest her weary bones. Especially if you insist on talking."

Hazel hobbled to the front of the store, locked the door, and flipped the sign from *open* to *closed*. "A woman is going to stop here in seven minutes, wanting advice on her love life, which is destined, by the way, to repeat itself over and over in a dissatisfying pattern that will one day be made all the more dissatisfying by her eventual understanding that she is the common denominator connecting all of these unsatisfying relationships. She's a deeply boring person filled with unrealistic expectations and a deep sense of entitlement. I'll be glad to miss her attempt at a walk-in consultation."

Hazel's cane tapped the floor as she passed Brawley and Sage and headed toward the back of the store. "Realizing the shop is closed, the woman and her girlfriends will go get ice cream instead, and that will give her more pleasure than I could have offered. Then she and her friends will climb back aboard their cruise ship and never return to Key West. Well, she won't return. But one of her friends, Brenda, will return in a few years with—"

Hazel's voice was lost as she passed with a rattle through a beaded curtain at the back of her shop and hobbled out of sight.

Brawley and Sage followed. Beyond the curtain, they passed into a short hallway with a door on each side. Hazel went straight ahead and opened a door onto a sunny alcove paved in mossy cobblestones and ringed in tropical plants spangled with colorful flowers. The space was circular, no more than ten feet in diameter, and hedged in by buildings and trees, the latter of which swayed in the breeze, dappling the intimate courtyard in an unsteady chiaroscuro of shifting shadows and sunlight. The soft wind breathed easily overhead, but here on the ground, the air was still, surprisingly cool, and redolent with sweet flowers.

"Don't you go trying to look up my skirt, sonny," the old woman said, and offered a dry cackle as she climbed with great caution into the alcove's only adornment: a hammock stretched between two palm trees. "Ah," Hazel said, shifting around and straightening her gown. "That's more like it."

"Before you peek inside," Sage said, "I need you to know that observing his truth might incur a degree of risk on your part."

Hazel grinned at that and said to Brawley, "Oh, she's a clever one, isn't she? How better to tempt an ancient Seeker than with a dire warning of requisite dangers? At my age, I crave dangerous information like a toddler craves sugar. Enough with your parlor tricks, my dear. Let me in."

Sage raised a hand. "Not quite yet, please. I need you to know that I'm serious."

"And I need you to know that while I might look like a senile old bat, I am not in reality a fool. I might not know anything about this young man, but context tells me plenty. I already know that you've fallen in love, Sage, and that your psi score has gone through the roof. I also know that you were somehow connected to the shooting today. I almost fell out of my hammock when that news hit me. Furthermore, I know that the dead men were acting on the orders of the psi mafia and that the Order is already involved."

"They are?" Brawley said.

Hazel nodded. "To a degree. I feel restraint there. A temporary restraint, however, hanging in the balance. But the local police have been redirected for the moment. Again, a temporary reprieve for those involved, but one that I can see, by your facial expression, puts you at some ease."

Brawley nodded. "Go ahead and do your thing."

"Do my thing," Hazel chuckled. She held out a gnarled hand. "Take my hand. Physical contact isn't strictly necessary, but it will make this easier, and besides, it's been years since I've held hands with a handsome young man."

Brawley grinned, liking this old woman. He took her hand and held it gently, mindful of the swollen knuckles, which could only mean arthritis.

Hazel shifted around and let her eyes flutter shut, looking like she was ready to nap.

Standing there holding her hand, Brawley was reminded powerfully of standing at his grandmother's bedside during her final moments. A rush of emotion surprised him, deep sorrow smashing him in the heart as he remembered his grandmother's passing and her last words to him.

By that point, most of the family had come to see his grandmother's cancer as a blessing in disguise. His grandmother had disappeared into Alzheimer's three years earlier, and by the time the lung cancer had arrived—a long overdue arrival, the doctor had joked, given her seventy-year habit of smoking three packs of cigarettes per day—his grandmother rarely recognized any of them and endured life in a state of constant agitation, grumbling her bitter mantra, *Just let me die. Just let me die.*

But unlike the rest of the family, Brawley refused to see the cancer as some kind of ironic angel of mercy come to end Grandma's suffering. At seventeen, he hated that cancer with a white-hot passion. His grandmother was the toughest person he had ever known, and coming from a bull rider out of Texas, that was saying something.

Grandma and her family had started the ranch,

scratching a living out of that unforgiving land. She'd been the oldest of *fifteen* siblings, hard as it might be to believe, and all fifteen preceded her in death.

Like so many barn cats, Grandma's brothers and sisters had lived violent lives and died violent deaths. They had been drowned in flash floods and shot in the wars; struck by lightning and stabbed in a poker game; thrown by horses and gored by bulls and bitten by rattlers. One had gotten rabies. Another disappeared into a tornado.

And though Grandma couldn't remember Brawley or his family, she remembered her past in sporadic bursts of shocking vividness, recounting these fantastic deaths in great detail and invariably expressing shame and wonderment to find herself the first of so many to die on her back in a bed.

To Brawley, Grandma Hayes was the soul of the family, the heart of the ranch, and spirit of the hard land he had come to love. Her father, brothers, and husband had all been bull riders, and as a girl, Grandma had climbed onto the backs of bulls until her father tanned her hide and then again whenever she thought she might get away with it. It was she who had first lifted Brawley onto the back of a calf and told him to ride. And a few months later, when Brawley got stomped for the first time and broke a rib, it had been Grandma who pushed the others away, pulled Brawley to his feet, and said, "Dust yourself off, cowboy. You're a Hayes. And that means you keep riding. No matter what."

That final, hot, high summer day in the back room of his grandmother's trailer, the air stifling with staleness and heat and worse smells than a gut-shot doe, seventeen-year-old Brawley held his grandmother's gnarled hand and cursed the cancer even as she faded away.

The family gathered around. Everyone was crying. Everyone but Brawley, that is.

Out of respect for his grandmother's commitment to

toughness, he had resolved to not shed a tear, not until she was gone at least. That was no easy thing. No easy thing at all.

Grandma's emaciated chest rose and fell. Her breaths were coming slowly and irregularly then, long and terrifying gaps stretching out between the rattling inhalations, each of which broke his heart afresh.

Then Grandma gasped sharply, and her eyelids opened. One eye stared through Brawley. The other drifted loosely, untethered in its socket.

The family tensed, sobbing, and for a brief, nightmare second, Brawley wanted to scream at them, he was so angry. Because he knew that they were hoping that it was over, that his grandmother had surrendered to death and would suffer no more.

He refused to welcome her end, regardless of the pain, not only because he loved his grandmother and couldn't imagine life without her but also because he knew that she would spurn their weakness and fight death every step of the way, kicking and biting and gouging eyes all the way to the grave.

At that moment, his grandmother's rolling eye recentered, and she stared up at Brawley with a clarity he hadn't seen from her in years. "Brawley," she croaked, using his name for the first time in many moons, "you hold on tight and ride hard, boy. Never quit. Never ever ever."

Even at seventeen, he understood she was talking about more than just bulls.

"I won't quit, Grandma. Not ever."

Then she died.

And Brawley had spent the rest of his life trying to honor his promise to her.

This memory struck him now with the power of a

charging angus, goring him straight through the heart with sorrow and love.

He staggered, releasing Hazel's hand, and almost fell. "What the hell?"

He didn't know what, precisely, he'd been expecting from this experience, but it sure as hell hadn't been this. He'd thought maybe Hazel would hold his hand then rattle off some neatly packaged information and be done with it.

"I'm so sorry," Hazel said, opening her eyes. "That memory had been crouched inside you, ready to come rushing out."

Brawley nodded, still rocked by the unexpected geyser of emotion.

"Your grandmother was quite a woman," Hazel said, "and fiercely proud of you."

"Thank you, ma'am."

She held out her hand again. "Would you still like to continue? You weren't the only one blindsided by your memory. It was so powerful that I glimpsed nothing else."

Brawley hesitated. If this experience was going to be like that, he wanted nothing to do with it. But his curiosity demanded that he proceed, especially if doing so might uncover not only his past but also something that could help him to keep his women safe.

Remembering his promise to his grandmother, he nodded to Hazel and gently took her hand once more. "Let's do it."

Hazel closed her eyes, and this time, he did, too. A second later, memories flowed over him. None had the complete-ness, clarity, or impact of the first. These snippets whipped by in incomplete flashes, and he barely registered snatches from the hours since his arrival in Key West. The taste of the hot banana peppers on his cold cut combo; the recoil of the Mac-10 in his hand; the shock he'd felt when Callie had lifted from the water and drifted toward him at the edge of Mallory Square.

Then his memories had gained speed, blurring into the past, and he caught only flickering glimpses of scenes hurtling back through time. Sitting in a Vegas parking lot, drunk off his ass, he and another rider splitting an apple pie, eating it with their hands like a couple of depraved savages; his mother drying her hands at the sink, singing softly and beautifully, a rare thing because his mother never wanted anyone thinking she was showing off, absurdly enough, the woman with the voice of an angel but as humble and plain-spun as a burlap dress; and way back when he was two or three, stumbling around the backyard and chasing Corky, the good-natured, snake-killing collie mutt that would later save his life when he was seven and a javelina charged out from a screen of prickly pear scrub, its curved tusks flashing like razor blades in the sun.

Faster and faster they descended into his past. Then they left his past, and tunneled into a deeper past, drilling beyond his birth and the boundaries of his life into a strange country where he could make neither heads nor tails of the slippery half-images blurring past.

Hazel pulled her hand free, and Brawley straightened, opening his eyes.

The old woman lay wide-eyed on the swaying hammock, clutching her chest as if she might be having a heart attack.

Hazel turned her gaze on Brawley. "You're a power mage," she said, her voice thick with awe.

He nodded. "That's what they tell me."

"This is what lit up the Latticework earlier today. You are a living, breathing power mage." She blinked and turned her head toward Sage, who had been watching and listening intently from beside Brawley and who slipped her hand into his now. "And that explains your power boost, Sage, and why the two of you fell in love though you only met today."

"Yes," Sage said.

"My, what a welcome to Key West you have had, Brawley," Hazel said, shaking her head. "And what a life to this point. A world champion. My oh my. But your grandmother never knew, did she?"

"No, ma'am. Did you see my past? My parents? My birth parents, I mean?"

"Your earliest days, both within and beyond the womb, were accessible to me, as was the time leading up to your conception. I saw your birth parents, their names, your true name, everything."

Brawley tensed, his curiosity boiling over. This was it.

"I saw them surrender you for adoption and understood their reasons for doing so and for shrouding you in the protective cloak."

"Who are they?" Brawley asked. "Who am I?"

Hazel frowned. "I'm afraid I can't tell you."

"Why?" Brawley and Sage said at the same time.

"Because everything I saw in your distant past was a lie. In all my many years of exploring the past, I have never seen such an elaborate and convincing cloak. I believed it all until what truth was available to me coalesced, and I was able to see the unreckonable dissonance between your would-be parents, a pretty pyrokinetic and a handsome telepath, in juxtaposition with the glaring fact that you are a power mage. Which meant that those two individuals couldn't possibly be your parents. Only a power mage can beget a power mage."

"Wait," Brawley said. "If the people in my past aren't my birth parents…"

"Constructs," Sage said.

Hazel nodded. "Complex and convincing fabrications.

They would have fooled me at any point in your life until you became a power mage earlier today. I have never seen such incredible illusory. Your true past—your birth parents' identities and motivations, along with your true name and bloodline—remain hidden behind a powerful shield. But that's not all.

"I now understand why your psionic ability took so long to emerge. Your strands had been psionically suppressed all these years. These powers never would have emerged if you hadn't suffered a traumatic injury months ago."

"Aftershock," he said. Then to Sage he explained, "A bull stomped me pretty good."

"Pretty good," Hazel laughed. "The bull snapped his neck, concussed his brain, and ended his career."

"Oh my," Sage said.

"Precisely," Hazel said. "But the accident—or, to use bull rider lingo, the wreck—also concussed him and fractured the suppressor. Did you feel anxious between the wreck and the Mallory Square incident?"

"Yes, ma'am."

Hazel nodded. "For one reason or another, your parents intended you to lead a normal life without psionics." She chuckled dryly. "But greatness finds a way."

"So my real parents locked up my strands, cloaked me, and still created a false past that obscured their identities, too. Why? Were they fugitives or something? I mean, they couldn't have known about the Culling beforehand, right?"

"It is very doubtful that anyone foresaw the Culling, or power mages would still walk the Earth," Hazel said. "Additional power mages, that is. We can't know why your parents disguised and limited you this way. Perhaps they were fugitives. Or maybe they suspected some unnamed tragedy and prepared for the worst. Or their love was forbidden, and they wanted to hide you away but also wanted to protect you. It's really impossible to know... for now."

"So, you can find out more?" Sage asked.

"Yes, I should be able to find out more. But it will take time. In the morning, after I rest, I will consult the Latticework. Return tomorrow afternoon. By that point, I should be able to answer the riddles of your curious past, Brawley."

"All right," Brawley said. "Thank you."

The old woman smiled sweetly. "No need to thank me, young man. This has been most exhilarating. A power mage. What an astonishing development. But we are not finished yet. We still need to look ahead.

"Also, Sage has provided a well-constructed cloak, but you shouldn't take any chances, especially now that someone at the Order is involved. I will hide you both behind a powerful cloak, and Sage, I will show you how to create similar shields, as well as mirror images to cast before you, should you suspect violence. You will then be able to cloak Nina. It is she, after all, that the Order is hunting."

"Thank you," Sage said.

"Of course, of course. With your new power, these will no doubt be quite easy for you now, child. And for you, Brawley, once you learn the basics. As I go about the action, I would like you to attend as well. That way, once you clear that firestorm of telekinetic energy in your mind, you will be able to progress rapidly as a Seeker. I've never seen someone with your psi score, and as a power mage, you will of course become even more potent. Which brings us to your future."

Taking his hand again, Hazel asked Sage to join them. "You should see this, too, dear, since your destinies are united now."

This time, Brawley could see nothing but churning darkness, like a wall of thick, black smoke roiling up from a million burning tires.

"A street sign," Sage said when the moment was over. "Nightshade Lane."

"Yes," Hazel agreed with a small smile. "That is the address I saw as well."

"But I don't have a number, a town, or even a state."

"Neither do I," the old woman said, and shifted her eyes to Brawley. "We could see very little of your future, likely because of your cloaks and because of the tremendous forces at play. But I have a very strong feeling that you should investigate this address."

Brawley nodded.

"Did you notice the sky, my child?" Hazel asked Sage.

Sage shook her head.

"Come and let us take another look together," Hazel said, grabbing Sage's hand.

Brawley watched the color drain from Sage's rapt face. Then she said, "The eyes..."

"A pair of gray eyes stares from the sky, searching for you," Hazel explained to Brawley. "Even now, wheels are turning. You have electrified the Latticework. People across the world are taking notice. Some already suspect that a new power mage has emerged. Soon they will come for you."

"Who will come for me?"

"All of them. Everyone."

"Time to grab the bull rope and hang on," Brawley said.

"I wish we could see what was going to happen," Sage said.

"As Grandma used to say," Brawley told them, "you don't gotta know what's coming down the pike. You just need the guts to handle it when it shows up."

15

Nina gripped her pulsing sex and bit down on the sweatpants, which she'd luckily shoved into her mouth just in time to muffle her cries of passion. Her body convulsed, shuddering through another orgasm, and she almost fell off the little bench, using one arm to catch herself against the wall of the little dressing room.

What the fuck?

She took a second to let the waves of climax recede, then opened her eyes to see her lust-crazed image in the full-length mirror.

Well, that was a first. Semi-public masturbation.

She didn't know whether to laugh or cry.

It was all so crazy. She was supposed to be shopping, not rubbing one out, but she couldn't stop thinking about Brawley. Making matters worse, she was also plagued by new, confusing, and exciting thoughts of Sage.

Then, while trying things on, Nina had noticed how wet she was. And swollen. And oh, even that soft touch had sent waves of pleasure through her body and filled her mind with lewd thoughts.

Almost without thinking, she'd pressed two fingertips to her glistening pearl.

And two feverish minutes later, she was biting down on the sweatpants and grunting through a powerful climax.

Now she was filled with confusion, shame, and excitement. She had to get ahold of herself.

After getting dressed, she took a deep breath, and headed toward the register. She had decided to grab a few things, including a pair of super cute pink running shoes.

Normally, she was careful with her spending, so this sort of shopping spree was a real rush. At the same time, she knew that some part of her was using the current situation to justify purchases she shouldn't make. Yes, she needed a workable disguise. But did that mean she needed to spend fifty bucks on new sneakers?

No.

But they were really cute…

Nina had the tab in her head and figured she could cover the bill with her own cash. It was sweet of Brawley to offer, but she wanted to pay her own way.

Perhaps that was a foolish, prideful compulsion, given how they felt about each other.

But hey, she thought, *in the immortal words of Popeye, I yam what I yam, and that's all that I yam.*

Her purchases would certainly be an improvement over her current get-up. The clothes Brawley had chosen were baggy and mismatched. Again, it was super sweet of him to take care of her, but she realized with a grin that his choices boded poorly for future birthdays and Christmases.

As she was passing the sporting goods, Nina spotted a ping pong table and headed that way for a look. Her dorky little half-brother, whom she adored with ever beat of her heart, loved ping pong. While other eleven-year-olds were playing team sports, obsessing over video games, or running around in packs looking for trouble, David spent his evenings at the community center, where he could play table tennis for free.

Apparently, he was pretty good, despite having to use the beat-up community center paddles against the custom paddles of the other tournament players. A couple of weeks ago, when Nina had pointed out the 1st place trophy on his windowsill, David had reddened and smiled, obviously embarrassed and proud all at the same time.

How she loved that kid.

She'd raved about how awesome that was, and David had promised to teach her how to play. But then David's mother, Beverly, had come home early from work, heard them talking, and stormed into the room. Good ol' Bev had kicked Nina out and threatened to call the cops.

What a bitch.

Of course, if the tables were turned, maybe Nina would be bitchy, too. After all, Beverly also loved David in her overbearing, highly annoying way. And when she looked at Nina, her maternal instincts probably flashed blood red.

Nina was Xander's other child, his first child, his child with a different woman, and it no doubt threatened and hurt Beverly that David and Nina got along so well.

None of this would've been such a big deal if Nina's dad and Beverly were still together, but Xander abandoned Beverly the way he always abandoned women, the way he always abandoned everyone. The great charmer, the king of the heartbreakers.

No one knew that more than Nina herself.

Every time Beverly saw Nina, she was undoubtedly reminded of her ex, whom she still chased for love and money, still obsessed with the man, despite his utter failure to pay child support or play much of a role at all in his son's life.

Which clearly made Nina's dad an asshole. But spend thirty seconds with the guy, and he'd have you smiling anyway. Even if he owed you a hundred bucks. *Especially* if he owed you a hundred bucks.

Because Xander Bartholomew Mack III was a top-notch Telepath with a flair for reading people and manipulating emotions. The guy could've been a movie star, a wildly popular politician, or the world's greatest therapist, helping the afflicted work through otherwise insurmountable emotional problems. Instead, he was a couch-surfing dead-beat with a great smile and a severe case of ADD—*Dad scrambled up?* he would quip. *Must be ADD!*—a telepathic conman living score-to-score and drinking his way to an early grave.

She loved and despised him in almost equal measure.

Almost.

But love won out by a hair, and that's all it took for Nina to keep going back to the man, to keep believing his shit, to continue hoping that this time, Dad really meant his gleaming promises, that this time, finally, he was going to change, going to become the man and the father they all knew he could be.

She would always love her daddy. Even if he constantly infuriated her.

Worse than fury, however, was fear. And if anything managed to push them apart, it would be her fear that he would suck her once more into his world of quick, nobody-gets-hurt-this-time scores. Or even worse—far worse, in fact—that he would rope David into that world.

Beverly always worried that David would be corrupted. But not by Xander. By Nina. Because Beverly, like the rest of the world, had no idea that Xander was the mastermind behind every crime Nina had committed.

Always suspected, never convicted, that was her dad. Like some weird, upbeat, criminal version of the perpetual bridesmaid. The guy could doggie paddle across an Olympic-sized pool filled with pig shit and come out smelling like fresh-baked cookies.

His stink all clung to Nina. At least as far as Beverly and the system were concerned.

Not that Nina could complain. She did the crime and did the time, and her father's involvement had nothing to do with that. Now, though, she had moved past all that, had left that world behind. And no matter what, she wouldn't let her dad pull her back in.

But who was she trying to kid?

What were shoplifting and B&E compared to the five counts of homicide?

That was different, she told herself. Those assholes had attacked her and Brawley. Self-defense was self-defense.

For an instant, she remembered Brawley crossing the driveway and putting the gun to the back of Gordo's head.

That wasn't self-defense.

Then, just as quickly, she realized that she didn't give a shit. The guy Brawley killed had come for her twice today. Besides, Brawley had warned him, had told him exactly what would happen if he came back, and the guy had come back anyway.

Nina shivered.

Then she shoved all that bad shit out of her head as best she could, focusing instead on something good.

David.

She would continue to visit her brother when she could and would continue to watch for any signs, no matter how small, that he was changing.

That's what she feared more than anything.

David had a fifty-fifty chance of opening a strand. In him, it would be a telepathic strand, of course, because unlike Nina's absentee, telekinetic mother, Beverly was all fuggle.

The closest thing the woman had to psionic power was her mind-boggling ability to jabber on and on and on.

That woman's all tits and talk, Nina's dad once told her when he was half in the bag and still running a tab at the Green Parrot. *The tits never lost their shine, but the talk sure did. And man cannot live on tits alone.*

So he'd tossed Beverly aside like an empty beer bottle. Of course he had. Because that's what Xander Mack did. He used people up and tossed them away. Despite the fact that Beverly also happened to come as a package deal with his son, David, who, heaven help the girls if the boy ever came to understand the power of his pearly whites, was looking more and more like his rakish father every day.

That burgeoning similarity also frightened Nina. Was David's million-watt smile merely a genetic call back or the sign of things to come?

If David developed telepathic ability, he would be immensely powerful. His life could be like a title of a self-help book: *Get Rich, Make Friends, and Date the Women of Your Dreams!*

With this power would come temptation.

Extreme temptation.

Ultimately, Nina didn't know whether she hoped her kid brother opened a strand or not. Telepathy could provide an easy, enjoyable life. Or it could ruin him.

Was psionic ability a blessing or a curse?

Both, she thought. *Of course it's both.*

But she had faith in her brother. David was good. Truly good. Kind and smart. An old soul. Power wouldn't ruin him, couldn't ruin him. He was, in his own quiet way, too strong for that.

Unless good old Xander found out, that was.

Because Dad would use David the same way he'd used Nina again and again.

She wanted to warn David but couldn't. At this point in time, David was a fuggle among fuggles. He had no clue about the psionic community, let alone the fact that his sister and father were part of it, and that he, himself, had a fifty-fifty chance of joining, too.

Unfortunately, if Nina tried to explain things to David now, he would think she was insane. It was hard enough, knowing your kid brother loved you *even though* you were an ex-con. And it was difficult knowing that David worried constantly over the possibility that Nina might do something and go back to jail. She couldn't have him worrying that she might be shipped off to the loony bin, too.

Picturing the boy's bright smile and thistle patch of wavy brown hair, her heart ached with love.

She walked past the ping pong table and studied the rack of paddles.

Beverly worked as a waitress at the Hard Rock Cafe. She earned enough to keep a roof over their heads, and David never went hungry, but there wasn't anything left over.

Having his own paddle would make David so happy.

Glancing at the prices, Nina winced. The nice ones started at forty bucks.

Nina stood there, biting her lip, studying the speed, spin, and control ratings like a woman trying to read Sanskrit.

For a second, she considered the basic model. Despite its attractive price tag, the thing looked cheap even to her untrained eyes.

She pictured giving David the cheap bat and knew beyond a shadow of a doubt that if she did hand her brother this piece of crap, he would explode with happiness and gratitude.

Fuck it, she thought, grabbing an eighty-dollar Stiga paddle. *Fuck it, fuck it, fuck it.*

She marched back to the shoe department, put the cute,

pink sneakers back on the shelf, and then backtracked through apparel, returning all the clothes except a sexy half shirt she'd found for three bucks on clearance.

She would go on wearing her combat boots and Brawley's ridiculous consignment shop disguise if it meant making David happy.

Shirt and paddle in hand, she headed to the register.

"You a big ping pong player?" the checkout guy asked.

"No," Nina said. "It's for my—"

Nina.

She jerked with surprise. *Shit,* she thought.

Nina, it's Dad.

I know who it is. Out of my head, Dad. Nina couldn't initiate telepathic contact or read thoughts, but once Dad opened a channel, she could hear his messages, and he could hear her thoughts as clearly as speech. *You know the rules.*

Rules. Even telepathically, he managed to infuse the word with scoffing laughter.

"Are you okay, Miss?" the checkout guy said, looking at her with concern.

"Yeah, sorry," she said.

Her father filled her head with laughter. *Catch you at a bad time, P Pop?*

P Pop was his nickname for her, stretching all the way back to when she was two and couldn't pronounce lollipop. An endearing nickname, sweet as candy on a stick, and one more trick he used to win her over again and again, despite her knowing better.

Don't P Pop me, Dad. You said you'd stay out of my head. You promised.

The checkout guy gave her a total. She didn't hear him and just handed the man all her cash.

Hey now, a man has the right to check on his daughter when he hears five people got whacked in her driveway. You okay, kiddo?

Nina crossed her arms. *I'm fine.*

You sure don't sound fine.

The checkout guy delivered his codified goodbye, handing her the bag, a receipt, and a few coins.

Boom.

Just like that, she'd reduced her life savings to a nickel and three pennies.

You're worried about money.

Out of my head, Dad, she growled internally, storming from the store.

You don't have to worry about money. In fact—

Really, Dad? Despite breaking the rules and barging into my thoughts, you were getting off to a refreshing start. For a second there, I thought you really were checking on me. You know, out of love or something like that. But it turns out you're just trying to recruit me again, huh?

Whoa there, P Pop, I was just going to say that I recently came into some money, and if you needed any help—

I don't want your money, Dad. Give it to David.

Nina didn't know if all telepaths could convey a sigh, but her dad sure could. Fucker could sigh like a champ. It annoyed the hell out of her. She was just about to tell him as much when his next transmission knocked her off balance.

Who is he?

Who?

Your new guy, that's who. Your thoughts are full of love.

Dad, stop. You promised you wouldn't spy on my thoughts, and my love life is 100% none of your business.

Hey, I did not spy on your thoughts. Can I help it if you're so gaga over some guy that he's stitched like bright red thread through all your thoughts? I want to meet him.

Like hell! There is no way I'm giving you the chance to ransack his thoughts.

P Pop, I only—

169

Stop with the fucking P Pop, Dad. You broke your promise again. Stay out of my head.

Sweetie, I heard about the shooting, and I was worried about you, okay? I love you.

Nina gritted her teeth. It was true. Despite all his bullshit, despite everything he had done and all the shit he was sure to do in the future, her father did love her. And she, God have mercy on her soul, loved him, too.

Because in life, we love our family. Even when they screw up over and over.

But she couldn't let her unconditional love trick her into ignoring reality.

Look, Dad, I appreciate you checking in, I really do. I'm okay.

What happened over there?

I don't want to get into it.

Is it over?

Yes.

Bullshit. You never could lie to your old man.

Well, that's my story and I'm sticking to it. Reaching the RV, she unlocked the door. *This is where we say goodbye, Dad.*

Come see me. I'm at—

I know where you are.

His voice chuckled with amusement in her mind. *My baby girl. Are you sure you didn't get some of your old man's telepathy?*

Yes, I'm sure. You're just predictable. And you haven't worn out your welcome at Captain Tony's yet.

He laughed again. *I miss you, kid. Come see me.*

No. I'm lying low. In fact, I'm heading out of town for a while.

Heading out of town? What about your parole officer?

Give me a little credit, Dad. I'm not stupid. I don't have another meeting for two weeks.

You're going with this Brawley guy?

Shit, Dad, stay out of it.

What the hell kind of name is Brawley, anyway? I want to meet him.

No. That's final. And stay out of my head. I mean it. I'll get in touch when I'm back in town.

No can do, P Pop. If you won't come and see me, I'm going to keep tabs on you, and there's nothing you can do about it.

I could hire a telepath to shield my thoughts.

More laughter. *Last I checked, black market mind mages charged more than eight cents.*

Dad! Stay out of my business!

Okay, okay. Just come over and see me, all right? Your old man wants a hug.

Nina sighed. She really didn't want to go see him. Up close, he would be able to read her thoughts with precision. But at the same time, she didn't want his third eye hitching a ride in her brain when they drove off in the RV.

That's it, he transmitted, his telepathic voice calm and full of good will. *Come see your old man before you go. Give me a hug and a little peace of mind, and I'll stay out of your business.*

That's what you said last time, but now we're having this conversation.

Hey, I mean it. Okay? Come see me.

Fine. But it has to be quick. I'm talking five minutes, tops. Now get out of my head, or the deal is off.

But—

No. Not another word. I'm serious. And no peeking, either. Whenever you start spying, I can feel you rooting around. It makes my brain itch.

All right. But hey, I know you're going to see David.

She clenched her fists with frustration.

Tell you what, her dad continued. *Swing by the bar, and we'll go together. He's really getting into this badminton thing.*

Ping pong.

Whatever. We'll surprise him. He'll love it. All three of us together.

Nina wanted to refuse, but at the same time, she also wanted her dad to be there for David, to start prioritizing the kid before it was too late. For both of their sakes. But of course, the idea also terrified her, because—

Wow, conflicted much?

Nina growled. It really sucked having a telepathic parent.

Oh, don't exaggerate. It's not that bad. Anyway, come on by, and we'll go see David together. See you soon, P Pop.

Nina stood in the silence of the RV, concentrating for a solid minute, trying to detect any unusual sensations in her mind. Finally, satisfied that her father really had exited her thoughts, she wrote a note to Brawley and Sage and laid his cash on the table.

For a second, she stared at the machine pistol.

She knew that Junior Dutchman and his crew were out there looking for her. And by looking for her, she meant hunting her down so they could blow her brains out.

Just fucking stellar, that.

If Junior's dad, the real Mr. Dutchman, had coordinated the hit, Nina would already be dead. The infamous *capo* of the local psi mob wouldn't have sent a truckload of half-cocked fuggles. He would have assigned his scary-ass bodyguard hitmen, Uno and Dos. There wouldn't have been any roaring SUV. Her head would have just exploded. Brawley's head, too, probably.

The thought chilled her.

It was stupid as hell, going into town now.

Not that she had to worry about Mr. Dutchman. The whole reason Junior wanted her dead was to keep her from saying something that would get back to Mr. Dutchman, keying him in to the fact that his shitbag son had been shaking down psi mages on the side and no doubt without paying his dad's cut.

Junior was a grasping wanna-be, pretending he could handle his own crew and call the shots. Normally, it was laughable. Now, it was a real problem.

In the wake of the botched hit, Junior would be desperate.

She just had to be extra careful, then. Sage had cloaked her, she was wearing her ugly-ass disguise, and the news still hadn't said shit about her.

She'd swing by Captain Tony's, grab her dad, and take him to the community center. Against her better judgment, she was excited to see her dad. She couldn't help it.

She was nothing if not loving, nothing if not loyal. Even when that loving loyalty had a way of dragging her through the mud, and the mud in question always ended up being full of broken glass.

She couldn't wait to surprise David with his new paddle. She'd let him know she was going out of town for a while, and then maybe she'd swing by Happy Times Chinese and tell Mr. Santini to go fuck himself, she quit.

That thought made her smile. Santini, who operated on a constant power trip and treated his employees like shit, would be livid. And that was that. The opportunity to watch a red-faced Santini sputter and curse justified any risk of heading into town.

But she wouldn't bring the machine pistol. It was compact yet still bulky enough to make carrying it under her sweats a real pain in the ass.

Besides, Brawley had filled her with so much power, she didn't need a gun. She could protect herself just fine, thank you very much.

Unless Junior and his psi-crew personally hit her this time. From behind. Without warning.

It was a risk she had to take.

She took a twisting path toward Old Town, swiveling through a circuitous network of alleys and less-traveled streets, keeping her hood up and her eyes peeled for trouble. She felt ridiculous and paranoid, all at the same time.

But when she reached Greene Street and strode into Captain Tony's, there was no sign of her dad.

He usually sat beside the tree, beneath the license plates and bras and signed dollar bills.

But he wasn't there. Or anywhere else around the bar.

She scanned the seating near the wall and glanced at the pool tables.

Her dad was nowhere to be seen.

Nina did a slow 360, double-checking the dim place, aware of men at the bar checking her out, despite her upturned hood, baggy sweats, and combat boots.

Maybe her dad was in the pisser. That had to be it.

She stood near the door to the men's room, waiting while one more Jimmy Buffet knockoff sang over the speakers.

Come with me, the singer crooned. *We'll sail the sea. Just the three of us. You and me.*

What kind of bullshit lyrics were those?

"Nina?"

She turned to see Steve, one of the bartenders looking her up and down with a confused smile. "Didn't recognize you for a minute. You look like Rocky training for a fight."

"Thanks, Steve," she said. "You really know how to sweet-talk a girl. Have you seen my dad?"

"Yeah, he was just here." Steve leaned forward, lowering his voice. "Hey, if you could say something to him, his tab is getting a little heavy. He's a great guy. I mean, everybody loves him. But—"

Whatever Steve said next, his words were lost to Nina, drowned out by the hammering of her heart. Xander Mack was many things, most of them bad, but he loved his daughter and cherished every second they spent together. He would never leave before Nina got here, not unless…

Stupid, she thought. *You are too stupid to even live.* "Steve, when did my dad leave?"

The bartender shrugged. "I don't know. Ten, fifteen minutes ago?" He grinned. "We're on conch time, remember?"

"Was he—"

Alone, she had meant to say.

But then her head filled with noise. Her father's voice, throbbing with fear and desperation, screaming in her mind, *Run Nina, run! They're coming for you!*

Leaving Hazel's shop was like exiting a dark, air-conditioned movie theater and stepping into a bright Texas afternoon. The difference was jarring, and nothing seemed quite real.

"Are you okay, husband?" Sage asked, slipping her slender arm over his shoulders.

"Yeah, I'm good. Just trying to wrap my head around everything she said. Sounds like we're in for a rough ride."

"Wherever you go, I will follow. As will Nina. You're our power mage."

"All right," he said.

For a moment, they walked in silence.

Balls was the one thing Brawley had always had, even when he was young and broke. But that was the problem right there, he realized. He would handle whatever was coming down the pike, but he couldn't help worrying about his women. It was easier to have big balls when you didn't have much to lose.

"I'll keep driving," he said, "but do me a favor, darlin. If it seems to you that I'm shoving my head up my ass, tell me."

Sage laughed. "I will always share my opinions, Master."

"What did I tell you about that Master shit?"

She eyed him overtop her sexy librarian glasses, smiling and batting her long lashes. "Perhaps you need to assert your dominance over me and really drill the lesson home."

Brawley pulled her close, liking the feel of her tiny waist beneath his fingers. "Now you're talking my language, sexy lady."

But then his nostrils were full of bad smells: blood and dirt, sweat and shit. A tremor rolled across his vision and through his flesh. Thousands of voices cried out, mostly muffled by the terrible ringing in his ears. White-hot pain raced across his neck, down his spine, and into his head.

Terror seized him. He was on the ground again. The ground was shaking, because Aftershock was pounding this way, looking to finish the job. Brawley had to get up, had to roll, had to run... but he couldn't move.

Reality rushed back in.

Brawley stood there, gasping, heart hammering, filled with panicky dread, his terror collapsing into a single image, which filled his heart and soul and named his fear even as Sage, her voice tight with apprehension, gave name to the object of his sudden concern.

"Nina," Sage gasped.

Yes, Nina. Something was wrong with Nina.

Sage said as much. "I can't see her. Not through the cloak."

Tourists flowed past where they had stopped on the sidewalk.

"Her nose ring," he said, remembering the psi sensor Sage had placed there.

"Yes," she said, recovering from her shock. "She's on Greene Street and moving fast. Coming out of Captain Tony's, near Mallory Square. She's really scared."

Rage burned to life in his blood. "Is someone chasing her?"

"I don't know," Sage said. "She's heading toward the center of Old Town."

"The community center," he said, and his gut told him yes, that was right. Nina had decided to go see her brother, and now she was in trouble.

"Come on," Sage said, moving in that direction. "We can find her. Just open your mind and concentrate on the question of Nina's whereabouts. You will sense her location. There is no better GPS system than a Seeker. Let's go."

"No," he said, pulling her to a stop. "I'll help Nina. You go back to your place and grab whatever you need, then head to the Publix parking lot and meet us back at the RV. Can you find it on your own?"

"Yes, but shouldn't—"

"Do it," Brawley said. Sage was brave enough, but she wouldn't be much use in a fight, and he didn't want to put her in danger, too. Besides, he suspected that they might need to pull up their tent stakes and hurry out of here sooner than expected.

He gave her a quick kiss and started running toward town. "See you at the RV," he called over his shoulder.

As he ran, Brawley did as Sage advised and focused on Nina's whereabouts. It was an easy thing to do since there was nothing more that he wanted in the world than to keep her safe.

No magical GPS system came to life, giving him directions or highlighting routes, but he did feel compelled to travel in specific directions.

Cut across this street, his mind proposed not in words but in notions. *Hang a left. Another. That way. That way. That way.*

He followed his gut, drawing closer and closer to Nina.

Then, as he was hustling along down a narrow street

flanking a deserted parking lot, a strong sense of foreboding passed over him like an icy wind, literally raising goose-bumps over his flesh.

Danger...

A motorcycle whipped past. Then its brakes screeched.

Brawley turned.

The rider, a burly guy on a crotch rocket, stopped in the middle of the street, spinning the bike around to face Brawley. A cloud of burnt rubber was drifting down the street, and the rider was reaching inside his leather jacket.

Brawley lifted his shirt with one hand and drew his XDS with the other.

They both fired at the same time.

Brawley felt something whip past the side of his face as the explosions of their gunfire echoed off the buildings lining the narrow street.

He stood his ground, firing then bringing the .45 back on target before squeezing the trigger again, aiming just below the concussive muzzle blasts of the rider's pistol.

One, two, three shots...

The rider jerked, spinning halfway around, firing into the sky as he tumbled from the bike. His pistol clattered away on the pavement.

The man's legs jutted out from behind the bike, twitching with convulsions.

Brawley checked his six.

At the far end of the street, people had stopped and were staring with horrified faces.

But he saw no bad guys.

Except the one flopping around like a slice of frying bacon on the other side of the bike.

Brawley moved in that direction, pistol at the ready. Yes, he'd struck the son of a bitch center mass, but for all he knew the guy was wearing body armor under that leather jacket, and Brawley wasn't taking chances. He didn't need someone on his back trail, gunning for him.

The guy's legs stopped shaking and drew slowly backwards, like roadkill curling up to die.

One could only hope.

Brawley circled around, trying to get a clear shot.

There was a loud whack, and then a wall of metal was rushing straight at Brawley.

If it weren't for his amazing reflexes, the bike would have cleaned him. But Brawley spun sideways like a bullfighter, and the motorcycle rushed past, missing him by inches.

The man had kicked the bike at him. What kind of strength would that take?

Brawley whipped back around, meaning to draw down on the freak, but apparently the man was just as fast as he was strong, because before Brawley could even level the XDS, what felt like a second onrushing motorcycle struck him hard, knocking him from his feet and sending his pistol skittering across the macadam.

His assailant paused for a second to straighten his back and roll his burly shoulders. His yellow t-shirt was splashed in crimson, blood draining from two separate holes, one in the gut, one high up the chest. "That hurt," the guy growled, swaggering forward.

Brawley hadn't been shot, but pain nonetheless filled his body. That son of a bitch had slammed into him so hard, it felt like he'd been stomped by a two-thousand-pound bull.

And he reacted just as he would have in the arena, telling his pain to fuck off and lurching to his feet. Only this time, instead of heading for an exit, he scrambled for his pistol.

He didn't make it.

The wall of force slammed into him again, bowling him over. He rolled across the pavement and slammed into the foundation of a brick building.

More pain, more problems. He lay crumpled on his back with his legs over his head. He swung his legs forward, trying to sit up, but then the guy was on him again.

The man's hand grabbed Brawley by the throat and hoisted him off his feet. The iron grip squeezed like a vice, cutting off Brawley's air. One sharp twist would rebreak Brawley's neck, dislodge the pin, and kill him.

Fuck that noise.

He grabbed the man's wrist but couldn't peel it from his throat. Looking down, he recognized the face leering up at him from inside the black helmet. It was one of the assholes who'd been shaking down the Cat Wizard with Junior Dutchman the night before.

The guy laughed nastily. "I thought that was you."

Brawley refused to let this bastard kill him. He had plans. First and foremost, helping Nina.

He lashed out with a hard kick and slammed his boot into the guy's nuts.

The guy didn't even flinch. He grinned, squeezing harder. "Never play poker with a man named Doc. Never shoot pool with a man named Ace. And never, ever fight with a Carnal."

In one, last, desperate effort, Brawley pushed. Not with his hands but with his mind.

All the pulsing power rushed from his mind.

There was a loud pop, and Brawley saw a bright flash of red before he instinctively slammed his eyelids.

The iron grip released him, and he fell to the ground, landing on his feet like he had so many times after getting tossed by a bull.

"The fuck?" Brawley panted, looking down at the man who lay on the sidewalk at his feet. One glance told him he didn't need to worry about the Carnal regenerating again.

The man's head was gone, helmet and all, reduced to a

thirty-foot smear of blood and shards, like a bug pulped across a windshield.

Brawley didn't hang around to study his handiwork. Somehow, his desperation had once again released a reflexive wave of force, only this time, instead of saving a cat, he'd saved himself.

He ran over, scooped up his XDS, and slipped it back into his holster. He was shaking badly. Not from fear but from having released such a powerful wallop of psionic force.

Then a funny thing happened. He felt an invigorating rush of energy plunge down through the crown of his skull and whip away into his mind.

For a quarter of a second, he felt a jolt of euphoria.

But then his big expenditure of juice hit him hard, and he forgot all about the quick rush of new energy. A beating heart of pain formed at the center of his brain, and the street seemed to tilt beneath his feet, threatening to topple him.

No, he growled, and caught himself.

He heard voices at the end of the alley and detected motion but couldn't sort it out.

Cops?

He didn't know.

He needed to pick up his brass, but with his trembling hands, shaky legs, and his vision now blurring, it would take him a day and a half just to pocket the spent casings.

But he couldn't leave those things lying there, covered in his fingerprints like so many calling cards. In his frustration, he imagined sweeping them from the ground...

And the little brass cylinders whipped into the air, winking with sunlight as they flew into his hand.

He shoved them into his pocket and sprinted away from the noisy end of the alley.

It seemed like voices were calling out from all directions.

Coming from both ends of the alley and calling down out of windows up and down the lane.

Brawley jagged to the right, throwing himself clumsily into a narrow alley between two buildings. His shoulder slammed into one of the walls, but he kept moving, kept putting one foot in front of the other, and stumbled down the alley toward the bright light at its end.

The heartbeat of pain in his head slowed as he struggled forward. The pain lessened. His body sense returned to him then. With it came his balance, and it no longer felt like the ground might catapult him into the sky. His vision cleared, and his stumble became a purposeful sprint.

By the time he broke out of the alley and into the crowded street beyond, his physical challenges had dwindled to a dull headache and another case of severe thirst. And of course, the pain remaining from his fight with the Carnal.

His throat hurt. His neck was badly bruised. And he was pretty certain the bastard had cracked a rib. Son of a bitch. If he hadn't already killed the guy, he'd go back and kill him all over again.

No one seeing him would have guessed he was hurt, though. Brawley had never understood why injured people complained or made faces. It didn't help a thing.

Besides, the damage he'd taken didn't matter.

Only Nina mattered now.

People cried out with surprise as he cut abruptly across the sidewalk and shot into the street. Drivers screeched to a stop, narrowly missing him, and horns blared as he crossed the busy boulevard.

Reaching the other side, he raced down the sidewalk, apologizing to those he bumped on his way, hung a hard left at the intersection and started pounding up the cross street as fast as he could.

Hang on, Nina. I'm coming, baby.

Nina ran.

The hat Brawley had given her flew off her head as she sprinted, weaving in and out of tourists, scared shitless and racing against time, her purple hair fluttering behind her like a purple streamer.

She cursed her stupidity. Why hadn't she warned her father? Because she'd been so rankled by his telepathic prying that it hadn't even occurred to her that he might be in danger. That's why. Stupid, stupid, stupid.

And now *they* had him.

She couldn't say who, exactly, had kidnapped her father, because his voice had broken off sharply immediately after screaming, *Run, Nina, run! They're coming for you!*

But she had an idea who *they* were. The thought chilled her, even as she sprinted at top speed through the sweltering afternoon heat.

Junior Dutchman and his crew had taken her father. How they had managed to strong-arm a telepath in a bar, she couldn't begin to imagine, but they had done it, and now they would squeeze whatever information they could from him. By any means necessary.

Anything and everything, including the existence and location of a person whose well-being she wouldn't have endangered for anything in the world.

So Nina ran. Not away, as her father had implored, but *toward*.

Toward someone.

David.

Even if Nina surrendered herself, Junior and his thugs would torture David for the simple pleasure of hearing him scream. And they would make her listen. Because brutal assholes like Junior understood and delighted in suffering. And Junior would know, the way a mean dog smells fear on a frightened child, that nothing would hurt Nina more than knowing she had caused her brother pain.

She had to reach David before Junior did.

Where was her father? Was he all right?

No, he wasn't all right. His telepathic scream had rung with terror—and then cut off abruptly. The man was clearly incapacitated. Psi-hobbled or knocked unconscious.

Or worse.

Please don't let it be that, she thought. She loved her father despite his many shortcomings, and even after all these years, some part of her still believed in him, still believed that he could change, that they could still establish the healthy, happy father-daughter relationship she had always dreamed of.

But now…

No.

She cut off that line of thinking. Yes, she hoped that her father was all right. But she couldn't do anything for him now. Yes, it was her fault that she hadn't warned him, but chastising herself further would only cloud her thoughts and hurt her chances of helping the one person she still might save.

She raced across the intersection, shouting apologies to the driver who almost hit her before slamming on the brakes and laying into the horn.

There, up ahead, she saw the lackluster brick building that had once been a school and now served as a community center meant to help kids like her brother to stick to the straight and narrow. Seeing a pack of kids loitering on the front steps, she felt a spike of hope. But then her head cleared, and she realized that these kids were much smaller than her brother.

He's always smaller in your head. Always younger.

Reaching the steps, she slowed to a fast walk. She was gasping for breath and soaked with sweat. She knew that she looked ridiculous in her disheveled and mismatched disguise but decided that she gave zero fucks.

The kids backed away, parting for her, and she raced up the steps and into the building. To the right, a cluster of parents stood inside the main office, talking.

From down the hall, she heard squeaking sneakers, the hollow thump of a basketball, and children's voices shouting. Then a whistle.

She hurried in that direction.

Please be okay, David. Please, oh please, oh please.

She rushed through the open doors of the lofty gymnasium. Her eyes whipped past the spirited game of half-court basketball, raced over a cluster of kids cartwheeling across gymnastic mats, and found the ping pong tables, two in total, looking somehow lost and pitiful shoved up against the shut-up bleachers.

Only two kids were playing ping pong.

Panic pierced her heart when she realized that neither of them was David.

Oh please, oh please, oh please...

But then one of the players, a short kid in a purple shirt, missed the table, and a third kid appeared, popping up from where he'd been sitting on the other side of the game, hidden from her view.

David snagged the errant ball, grinning like a madman, and her heart nearly broke in two.

Oh, thank you, thank you, thank you.

"David," she called, surprised to feel the burn of seeping tears at the corners of her eyes.

David looked like somebody had goosed him. Then he smiled uncertainly. "Nina? What are you doing here? Is everything all right?"

The other kids turned around and stared at her. Not just the ping pong players, either. The aspiring gymnasts had paused their tumbling and stood now in a whispering huddle, watching her.

Were they staring because she looked so crazy in her rumpled sweats, combat boots, and purple hair? Or were they staring because everyone knew that poor David's older sister was an ex-con?

She didn't give a shit one way or the other. Not now, anyway. Right now, all she cared about was David's safety.

"Yes," she lied. "Come on. I need to talk to you for a minute. Alone."

David hesitated, and she saw something in his green eyes that nearly broke her heart.

Fear.

Her kid brother, whom she loved more than anything in the world, and who loved her just as fiercely, was nonetheless frightened to go someplace alone with her.

Fucking Beverly.

"I'm supposed to stay here," he said, blushing.

"Okay," she said, and turned to the other two players. "You two get lost. Now."

The kids dropped their paddles and hurried away.

Her brother watched them go, looking confused and uncomfortable.

"Give me a hug," she said, and pulled him into a sweaty embrace. When she let him go, she saw that his face was red.

So I don't just scare him. I embarrass him, too.

But none of that mattered now.

"Are you all right?" David asked again. "You're not in trouble again, are you?"

"No," she said, wishing it were true, wishing she could be the older sister he deserved. "Not really."

"Nina," he said, his face collapsing with worry. "What's going on? Is Dad okay?"

Her first instinct was to lie in yet another attempt to protect David from the ugly side of the world, but that was no longer possible.

Because the ugly side was coming for him now.

"I don't know if Dad's okay," she said. "Listen, David, some bad people have taken him."

"What do you mean?" David whined. He started rocking back and forth with his skinny arms crossed over his chest.

Nina didn't have time to comfort the kid. She glanced nervously over one shoulder. Any second now, Junior might come racing through those doors. "You have to get out of here. Don't look at me like that, David. You have to leave. Don't go home. Go to a friend's house, okay? And don't leave a note. Call your mom instead and let her know. Both of you should stay someplace else for a few days, all right? And don't go to school, either."

"You're not making any sense," he said.

"I'm making total sense," she said. "You just don't want to hear it. Look, David, I'm sorry to put you through this.

I'm sorry for a lot of things. But you have to believe me. These people, they will hurt you and your mom if they find you."

All the color drained from her brother's face. She hated to frighten him like this, but she had to.

"I don't understand," David said, his voice trembling now. "Who are these people? Why would they want to hurt us? What did you do?"

"I didn't do anything," she said. She wished she could stop time and explain everything. All of it.

Why hadn't she just told him everything a long time ago? He was a smart kid. He could've dealt with it. And if he'd looked at her like she was crazy, she could have given him a demonstration. So why hadn't she?

Because she'd been afraid, that was why. Afraid he might look at her like she was crazy. Afraid that he was fragile. Afraid that his love for her was fragile. Afraid that, by unveiling the secret world to which she belonged, she might somehow doom him to a similar fate.

So many fears and so much bullshit.

The facts were the facts, and she couldn't hold back now. "Dad and I have powers, David."

His eyes went wide. "Powers? Like super powers?"

"Yes," Nina said, already regretting this detour. Why hadn't she stuck to the basics? Why had she dropped this on him now?

Because she had to. Because she couldn't hide the truth from him any longer. By trying to protect him, she had almost gotten him killed.

"We have powers, and there's a good chance you have powers, too. If you do, they won't show up for a couple of years. You'll be able to—" But she slammed on the brakes. No sense going there now. "I'm not crazy, David. And I'm not kidding. But these bad people, they're after me, and I think they have Dad, and they're probably going to look for you next. And if they find you—"

"Stop," David said, and burst into tears. "Please stop. You're scaring me."

Shit, she thought. Shit. Shit. Despite her best intentions, this was all going sideways at 110 miles per hour.

She hauled him into a hug. "I'm sorry, David. I'm really sorry. I hate to scare you, but I have to scare you, because if you don't take me seriously or if you underestimate these people, they will do bad things to you. Worse things than you can even imagine." She released him. "Stop crying now. Take a deep breath. That's it. Everything's going to be okay."

"No it isn't," he said, whipping his head back and forth. "Things with you will never be okay, because you're always in trouble, and now you got Dad into trouble, and—" His lament crumbled into a sobbing fit.

Nina cast another glance over her shoulder. No Junior, no thugs. Not yet, anyway.

The basketball game had broken up, and the teen counselor was leading the players out of the room. The gymnasts were nowhere to be seen.

She seized her brother by the arms. "We have to get out of here. Now."

He shook free, surprising her with his strength. "No," he said, and his voice broke, going high and tinny with terror. "I'm not going anywhere with you."

His look of terror made her feel like crying. But she couldn't cry. Not now. There wasn't time to cry. She had to get him out of here before it was too late.

"Listen to me, David," she said. "I know I sound crazy, but I love you, and I need you to listen to me. I would never hurt you. You know that. But if you don't come with me now, other people will hurt you. Badly. Do you understand?"

She reached for him, but he backed away and tripped over a bag and fell hard on his ass. He burst into fresh tears.

Oh, she had fucked this up so royally. It was fear that had done it. Fear, her old enemy, sticking it to her again. "Just forget what I said about super powers, okay? We can talk about that later." Even as the words left her mouth, she knew they only made things worse, only made her seem crazier. "You just need to come with me now. That's it. All right? We have to go someplace safe before it's too late."

He shook his head and sobbed.

For a second, all she could do was stand there clutching her bag, paralyzed by her inability to unfuck this situation.

Then she remembered what was in the bag she was holding and impulsively tossed it in his direction. "Here," she said, trying to sound cheery. Unfortunately, she overdid the fake enthusiasm and her voice came out in a wild chirp, "I got you a paddle!"

David flinched as the bag landed in his lap. His eyes were shut tightly, and snot and drool were draining from his mouth and nose.

"Miss?" a man's voice called behind her.

She whirled, hackles raised, ready to kill for her kid brother.

An older man with a huge keyring on his hip stood just inside the door, holding a broom in both hands. Behind him, she saw a cluster of kids watching with worried faces.

"Miss, can I help you?" the custodian asked.

"No, we're fine," Nina said, trying to make her voice as natural as possible. "This is my brother," she said in an awkward half-explanation that she instantly understood did nothing to make the situation better. "We're fine. Really. Thanks."

"Miss, could you come with me to the office, please?" the

man said. He stepped forward, a worried look on his face. "This area is for the children, and—"

"Where is David?" a high-pitched voice demanded. "Where is my baby?"

And then—*fuuuuuuuuck*—Beverly stormed into the gym.

David's mother's eyes burned with fear and rage. Her head was tilted to one side, pinching a phone to her shoulder. "You! Get away from him." She hurried past the custodian, pointing at Nina. "Yes, ma'am," she said into the phone. "It's her. Nina Mack. She's not supposed to be here." Twisting the phone away, she shouted at Nina, "You're not supposed to be here!"

"Bev, I can explain," Nina said, biting back her anger. "David is in danger."

"You get away from my son," Beverly said. "David, sweetie are you okay?" Then, speaking into the phone again, she said, "Okay, yes, ma'am. I'll tell her, Ms. Jackowski."

Fuck, Nina thought. Ms. Jackowski was her parole officer.

"You are in big trouble," Beverly said. "I have your pa—"

"Shut up!" Nina shouted, and with a flick of her mind, she ripped the phone from Beverly's stupid hands and whipped it across the gym, where it smashed against the block wall and fell in pieces to the wooden floor.

Beverly slammed to a stop. Her mouth fell open.

"Everybody out!" Nina shouted, and turned her focus to the custodian, who, propelled by a wall of invisible force, slid slowly backwards out the door, which slammed shut behind him. The other doors followed suit, slamming shut one after another.

Nina had fucked this up beyond all belief, but it was too late to change that now, too late to rein it in. She had to protect her brother, even if it meant he would spend the rest of his life thinking of her as a monster.

But she had to hurry. The cops were undoubtedly

speeding this way. She had to get her point across before they arrived.

And then she laughed, realizing she had inadvertently achieved her goal. In a few short minutes, this place would be swarming with cops and parents. Junior would take one look at the commotion and turn the other way.

"Why are you laughing?" Beverly demanded. Apparently, some part of her brain had conveniently rejected the smashed phone and slammed doors in a kind of defensive denial. "Are you on drugs?"

"No," Nina said, and laughed again. She couldn't help it. This whole situation was so crazy, so fucked up, and at the same time, she was so relieved that David would be okay. At least for now.

The thought of what could still happen later sobered her instantly.

"Listen to me, Bev," Nina said. "This is serious. There are bad people looking for David. They will hurt him if you go home in the next few days. When the cops get here, tell them you need protection."

"This has to do with the shootings, doesn't it?" Beverly said. Apparently rediscovering her anger, she strode forward. "Those five people on the news. The ones shot to death in your driveway."

"Yes," Nina said. "It does. And if you don't do as I say, you are going to die, too."

Beverly's eyes went wide. "Are you threatening me?"

"No. I'm warning you. There's a difference."

Beverly's face had shifted through deep red to dangerous purple. She advanced with her fists balled. "You leave us alone, you little bitch!"

And suddenly, Nina had had enough. Because while yes, she was one of the most powerful telekinetics in the nation, she was also a twenty-two-year-old girl who'd spent half of her life eating Beverly's shit just so she could spend time with David.

Now lines had been crossed.

"You're just like your father," Beverly sneered, drawing back a fist. "You think you can come into our lives whenever you please and—"

Beverly stopped, locked in place by a gigantic, invisible hand. When she started to protest, a smaller invisible hand covered her mouth.

"You listen to me, Bev," Nina said. "I've always been nice to you. I've always tried to get along, because I wanted to see David without you being a pain in the ass. But you know what, Bev? I am now officially sick of your shit."

She gave the big hand a little squeeze, not enough to damage Bev but enough to get her message across. Emphatically.

"But what I really care about is David," Nina said.

She could hear her brother whimpering behind her, and she hated that she had screwed up like this, but everything she had done, she had done to protect him. Sometimes, we have to act like monsters to save the ones we love.

"Take him someplace safe," she said. "Out of town if possible. This should all blow over in a few days, but stay on your toes just in case, all right? And when this does blow over, let's pretend none of this ever happened. I'll visit David, and everything will be fine."

She gave the invisible hand one more squeeze. "One more thing before I let you go, though. And I want you to remember this forever, okay, because it's super-duper important. I know you hate me, and that's fine, but do not fuck with me, Bev, or I will make you suffer."

18

Junior Dutchman stood a few feet back from the cleaning station, gritting his teeth every time his father slapped another half-fileted grouper down on the board. Junior didn't mind blood. He just didn't want any on his new Robert Graham shirt, which had cost him three hundred bucks.

Meanwhile, his father, having just returned from a fishing trip, was wearing a ratty t-shirt and cargo shorts streaked in gore. With his blurry jailhouse tattoos, deeply tanned skin, and the cigarette dangling from his lips, Roland Dutchman, Senior, looked more like a professional fisherman than the capo of Florida.

The impression was exacerbated by the attire of Senior's constant companions, Uno and Dos, a pair of top-notch trig-germen on semi-permanent loan from Mr. Valdez himself. Uno favored bowling shirts two sizes too large. Dos wore tank tops two sizes too small.

When Junior first met the hired killers, he'd cracked on their clothes, but they had given him dead-eyed stares, the men having no sense of style or humor. But they were good at their work. That was for sure.

At this moment, that was an uncomfortable truth.

Junior waited, doing his best to seem cool and confident. You couldn't let Senior see you sweat, no matter what.

Senior tossed a tangled wad of fish guts off the dock. Down in the water, the massive tarpons trashed, fighting over the scraps. Then the man finally looked up from his bloody workspace and bored his orange-brown eyes into Junior's.

"Five of your men were killed," Senior said, "and you have no idea what happened?"

Junior wished he'd left his shades on. If he put them back on now, however, his father would notice. "Only three of those guys worked for me. The other two—"

"A pair of cut-rate freelancers out of Boca Raton," Senior interrupted. Grabbing another fish by the tail, he slid his thin blade up its body, peeling flesh from bone. "I know that much already and will know much more soon, I assure you. Because, my ambitious son, that is your job when you run the big show: knowing everything."

Junior nodded. Better to keep his mouth shut at this point, see where his father went with things. The man's icy calm, intense stare, and reputation for turning people into chum had a way of unnerving those he questioned.

"Now, humor me son, and give me your best guess. What were Gordo and the others doing with these black market mercenaries? Or do I have to have Gabriella ransack your mind?"

Junior raised one eyebrow and tried to look cool, glancing between his father and the pale woman standing several feet beyond the cleaning station. She was likely trying to avoid getting fish guts on her classy charcoal business suit. Gabriella was easy enough on the eyes in a corporate kind of way, but truth be told, she scared the shit out of Junior. The absolute last thing he needed was a Bender peering through his skull and relaying his thoughts to his father.

Because Junior *did* know what had happened to his men, including the two mercs from Boca. But if his father knew that, Senior would have his head. Junior didn't think his father would literally kill him for shaking down psi mages on the side, but Junior would lose any chance of ever succeeding his father as capo.

And that, ladies and gentlemen, would be totally un-fuck-ing-acceptable.

Junior had worked too hard and hustled for too long to see it all blow up in his face now.

If Gabriella did hack his brain, she wouldn't get shit. Junior had paid plenty to shield his mind from Seekers and Telepaths. But the discovery of those shields would trigger Senior's suspicious nature and likely drive the man to have Uno and Dos conduct an old-school, non-psi interrogation.

And that would not do, because Junior had grown attached to his fingers, thank you very much.

So Junior did his best to look cool, saying, "If you don't believe me, go ahead and tell her to take a peek, but if you can't trust your own son, how does that look?"

"The day I need your advice on running this organization," Senior said, hurling another rat's nest of bloody intestines into the water, "cut me up and feed me to the tarpons."

Gladly, Junior thought. As was his habit, he analyzed the situation, imagining the best way to kill everyone. He would hit Uno with a psionic blast, then go for his Glock, trying to get the drop on Dos. He would have to backpedal as he fired in case his father came at him with that skinny-bladed filet knife. It was easy to forget that Senior had started as an enforcer on the streets of Miami before climbing the ranks of the psi mafia.

Gabriella cleared her throat and started squirming, straightening her skirt and blouse with a glazed look in her big eyes. Then her expression cleared, and she said, "There has been an incident."

Junior listened as the woman explained that his closest friend, Marco, had just been shot to death.

Shit. That was inconvenient. It had taken a long time to recruit Marco and build the big Carnal's trust. Replacing him would be a major pain in the ass.

Junior had to find Nina. Had to find her and kill her before his father found out that she was involved.

"Who killed Marco?" Senior said, his voice burning low and dangerous.

Gabriella's eyes went out of focus again. For a time, they stood there waiting for her to respond. Senior watched with his mouth all puckered up like a bullet wound. Uno and Dos lazed there, looking bored.

Junior was tense, worried that she'll mention Nina. Reflexively, he drew up a bundle of a force.

"Marco was driving past on his motorcycle," Gabriella said, narrating the information was apparently delivered to her via the thoughts of someone in the know. "The other man was walking on the sidewalk."

Man, Junior thought, and his grip on the automatic relaxed.

"They recognized each other," Gabriella continued. "Both opened fire."

"I didn't ask for a play-by-play," Senior said. "Who was he?"

Gabriella shook her head. "We don't know."

Senior snarled with frustration. "Get Bostic. Tell him I need to know—"

"This is all coming from Mr. Bostic, sir. Whoever killed Marco is cloaked."

"And I pay Bostic extravagantly to unravel cloaks."

The pretty Bender frowned. "My apologies, Mr. Dutchman. Apparently, the cloak is very strong. It's the work of a powerful Seeker. Mr. Bostic can only see the man's basic shape. He is tall and lean. And very fast."

"Faster than Marco?" Junior said incredulously.

Gabriella shook her head. "No. But very fast all the same. Decisive. Clearly comfortable with violence and more than competent with firearms. Marco had the upper hand, but the man killed him with a psionic blast. An extremely powerful psionic blast."

"A powerful telekinetic who's good with guns and heavily cloaked?" Junior said, turning to his father, who was nothing if not paranoid. "Sounds like a professional."

Senior looked thoughtful for a second, his dangerous eyes narrowing slightly. Then he nodded. "Perhaps the psi cartel is making its move."

Yes, Junior thought with relief. His father's paranoia had taken the bait. Time to set the hook, even if it meant looking stupid. "They wouldn't dare move on us."

Senior turned to him with a look of contempt bordering on disgust. "Sometimes, it is difficult to believe that you are my son. Of course they would dare to move on us. Gabriella, tell Bostic to focus his surveillance on the psi cartel. If he feels anything—*anything*—I want to know. Everyone else, we are on high alert."

"Mr. Bostic says he will try, sir," Gabriella said. "But the Latticework is still buzzing with the aftershocks of today's big event, so surveillance at this range might prove difficult."

The Latticework is still buzzing, Junior thought with another shade of relief. Apparently, Seekers around the globe were convinced that a monumental power shift was on the horizon. Some of the kooks even thought a new power mage had emerged. Whatever the shift was, most agreed that it was happening here, in the Keys.

A new thought occurred to him as his fingertip traced the trigger guard of the snubnose .38 in his pocket. Was the big power shift rocking the Latticework foreshadowing an opportunity for Junior? Was it time to make his move?

"Talk to Bostic and find a way to surveil, Gabriella," Senior said, "or you both can find yourself a new employer."

"Yes, sir," Gabriella said, looking nervous. She didn't need precognitive powers to know what *find yourself a new employer* meant in Senior's world.

As if on cue, one of the big tarpons splashed loudly, wanting more scraps.

"Mr. Bostic senses a big storm approaching," Gabriella said with a hallowed voice.

Junior wondered if she was telling the truth or just trying to distract Senior.

"A big storm with major ramifications to this organization," Gabriella continued. "And you, Junior, will be at the center of it."

"Good," Junior said, faking a smile. "I'm ready to step up."

"Ready to step up," Senior said with a dubious tone. "What was Marco doing?"

Junior did his best to look confused. "How the hell should I know? I'm not a Seeker."

"But he was your friend," Senior said. "Your constant companion."

Junior shrugged. "He'd been acting a little odd lately."

"Odd how?" Senior said.

Careful now, Junior thought. "I don't know. Just weird. Busy, I guess. Like he always had someplace to go lately."

"Such as…"

Junior shrugged again. "How am I supposed to know?"

Senior rapped his curved blade sharply against the bloody counter. "It is your business to know."

"All right," Junior said. "I'll hit the street."

"Do that," Senior said. "Don Valdez will be in touch soon about this big psychic event and the two gunfights. I need answers. And if the don doesn't like those answers, he will kill and replace all of us by the morning tide."

As Junior walked away, he couldn't help but grin. His father was uncharacteristically rattled, paranoid about the psi cartel and feeling pressure from Don Valdez.

This could be it. This could be his moment of ascension.

Then he noticed a dime-sized spot of fish blood on the cuff of his new shirt. "Fuck."

————

TWENTY MINUTES LATER, JUNIOR WAS PACING JUST INSIDE THE door of Rick's apartment. He generally avoided the place, which was stacked floor to ceiling in machines. And not just computers and phones, like your garden variety Gearhead. Rick had all types of shit piled up in there. Microwaves, televisions, printers, everything. In front of his couch, where a sane person might have a coffee table, Rick had a fucking car engine.

You'd think a guy who worked with machines would be able to understand something as nuts-and-bolts simple as life and death, but old Rick was having a hard time wrapping his head around the subject.

"Dead?" he asked again. "Marco?"

"Yeah," Junior said, "dead. Now come on. This place makes me feel like I'm covered in ants."

Rick blinked, his eyes passing over the stacked machines as if seeing them for the first time. "I can't believe it. Marco."

"Enough," Junior said. "He's fucking dead, okay? And

unless you want to join him, get off the couch and come with me now."

That got Rick moving. The kid always had been malleable. Which made no sense. Shit, if Junior could hack people's phones and computers with his mind or make their engine seize up while they were flying down the highway, he wouldn't take shit off anybody.

But Rick was a pussy. And once a pussy, always a pussy, no matter how much power a guy like Rick gained.

They crossed town to the crime scene. The cops had the place roped off pretty good, so they couldn't get close, but that was okay. Rick had line of sight. That's all that mattered.

The skinny little technopath stared up at the security camera mounted across from where the detectives were doing their forensic dog and pony show. Rick's eyelids blinked rapidly. Junior could all but hear shutter clicks.

"Got it," Rick said with a smile.

"And?"

"Give me a second to play it back." Rick held out his phone, and the two of them watched together as the hacked security cam footage played back the fight. "Oh, Marco. Man, I feel like I'm going to puke."

The puny technopath staggered to the sidewalk's edge and gagged. Junior yanked Rick's phone from his hands and did his best to ignore him while playing back the footage.

It made no sense. The mystery man was all static.

"Dude, stop whining," Junior said. "What's wrong with the footage? How come we can't see the other guy?"

Rick shook his head. "Some kind of powerful cloak."

Junior cursed. Gabriella had said the cloak was powerful. Strong enough, it appeared, to block not only Seekers but also obscure his identity on film. "All right. Burn it."

Rick nodded. A second later, the security camera popped,

sending a spray of sparks raining down from where it was mounted atop the brick building.

Crucial, that. It wouldn't do, letting the fuggle cops see too much.

Junior did a slow 360, then nodded to the security cam in front of the bodega across the street. "Anything?"

Rick studied the camera for half a minute and shook his head.

"Come on," Junior said. "We'll keep checking every exit until we find this asshole."

Rick nodded. With his long skinny neck and big eyes, he looked like a chicken trying to lay an egg. "And then what?"

"You know what." Today had really kicked Junior in the nuts. He'd lost four men. Six counting the triggermen from Boca. But he wasn't nearly as stupid as he led his father to believe. He still had his four best soldiers, and they were geared up, waiting for the call.

"There he is," Rick said, staring at a streaming cam outside a bar facing the exit of an adjacent alleyway. "He went west."

"All right," Junior said, clapping his small friend on the shoulder. "Burn it and keep checking cameras. Hunting season on assholes is officially open."

19

Brawley reunited with Nina just as she emerged from the community center, and they hustled together across town.

Nina was so upset about her dad, her brother, and losing her shit with Beverly that they were halfway back to the RV before Brawley even had a chance to mention that he'd killed a Carnal.

That sent Nina into a tailspin of fresh anxiety.

The guy's name was Marco, she explained. He was Junior Dutchman's best friend.

Then, as they were hiking along North Roosevelt, Nina said, "If Junior hurts my dad, I'll kill him."

Brawley gave her shoulder a squeeze. "And I'll help you."

He hoped her dad was okay and hoped she would be able to patch things up with her brother, but right now, his primary worry was keeping his women safe and getting the fuck out of Dodge before it was too late.

The fight with Marco would bring serious heat.

And right now, he just wanted to get on up the road and

find Nightshade Lane, wherever the hell that was. This Seeker curiosity thing sure was a bitch and a half.

He wished Sage was with them. Apparently, her apartment wasn't far from Publix. Maybe she would be waiting for them at the RV.

Once they were together, they would jet.

But when they reached the RV, Sage was nowhere to be seen.

Brawley opened the fridge and grabbed them both a beer. After blasting Marco, he had a headache and was once more dying of thirst, though he was in much better shape than he had been following the Mallory Square debacle. After knocking back a beer, he felt even better.

Nina paced back and forth, sipping her beer and muttering about how they were screwed. "And then someone's going to send fucking Remi after us, I just know it."

Brawley reloaded his XDS, made sure the other firearms were ready to go, and popped another beer.

Nina stopped pacing abruptly and said, "Dad?"

Brawley whipped around but saw they were alone.

Nina's sweet features twisted with concern. "Dad, I can feel you in my brain. Are you okay?"

Then Brawley understood. Nina's missing father was a telepath. He was reaching out to her now. Brawley braced himself, waiting for her dad's captors' ultimatum.

Nina relaxed visibly. "I was worried the psi mafia had you. Wait… what?" Her eyes narrowed. "Who are you with, Dad? And no, I'm not telling you where I am."

Nina frowned, hurried past Brawley into the kitchen, and started rooting through the pantry.

"No, Dad, you listen to me. Jamaal's gotten inside your head. You believe that shit because he *made* you believe it. No. I'm not telling you where I am. Listen to me, you have to get away from him as fast you can, no matter what he's saying."

She pulled out the aluminum foil and pulled off a large sheet, which she started forming into a bowl. "Nope. Not going to tell you, Dad. Stay out of my head. Jamaal is a liar. No. That's my final answer. I love you, Dad, but I have to go. This is me hanging up."

And she slammed the silver bowl down on her head like a beanie cap.

"The Order has my dad. This old ass cop, Jamaal. He's a Seeker. Busted me twice. I know he's planting false notions in Dad's head, making him think that figuring out where I am is the only way to save me from certain death." She snarled with frustration. "Jamaal's like a Southern sheriff and his pack of bloodhounds all rolled into one. What? Why are you looking at me like that?"

Brawley pointed to the hat. "That's how you block a telepath?"

Nina blushed and adjusted the shiny cap. "Yup. Turns out all those conspiracy theorists weren't so crazy after all. Aluminum foil blocks mind mages. Up the road, we can stop in Marathon. I know a semi-shady telepath up there who would put a shield on me for a few thousand dollars."

"All right," Brawley said, and couldn't help but grin. "You going to wear the hat until then?"

"Of course I'm going to wear the hat," she said, pulling it down more tightly as she paced away. "Go ahead and crack your jokes. At least my name isn't Brawley."

"Good comeback," he said. "It's even funnier in the hat."

She slapped her ass. "Bite me, cowboy."

Going to a window, she pulled aside the curtain and stood on tiptoes, looking out into the parking lot.

He wished she would spot Sage coming this way.

Instead, Nina gave him a lopsided grin. "Happy day-versary."

"Huh?"

"The sun is setting. We've officially known each other for twenty-four hours." Beyond her, through the tiny space where she'd pulled the curtain aside, he could see the orange light of sunset.

"That was one hell of a day," he said.

"You can say that again," she said, coming away from the window. "Yesterday, I was a delivery girl for a Chinese restaurant, doing my best to stay out of trouble. Now I'm unemployed, my dad is helping the Order to find me, my brother thinks I'm crazy, his mom called my parole officer, and the psi mafia wants to kill me. Oh, and I'm eternally bound to a Seeker and to a power mage who has wasted half a dozen people today." She looked down at the sweats and combat boots. "Meanwhile, I'm wearing the ugliest disguise in the world and sweating like a whore in church."

She unzipped the turquoise hoodie and let it drop to the floor. She wore no t-shirt underneath. Just a red bra. And once again, her perfect body glistened with a fine sheen of perspiration.

Despite all that had happened, despite all that could happen, Brawley felt himself growing hard again. Nina looked incredibly sexy, and he'd been hornier than hell ever since she'd opened his strand. Even hornier since Sage had opened his second.

Nina shoved down her yellow sweatpants almost franti-cally, then wobbled back and forth, looking lovely standing on one leg and trying to pull her sweatpants over her combat boots. She pulled the first pant leg free, switched stances, and growled as she pulled the other half of her sweatpants labori-ously over the boot.

By the time she'd finished, Brawley had iron in his pants.

Then she stood there in a red bra, matching panties, combat boots, and her ridiculous headwear.

The sight of her made him throb with desire.

"Ugh," she said, sounding exasperated. "My life is a dumpster fire." She growled again, clenching her fists and glaring at Brawley with her mismatched eyes. "I'm wearing a tinfoil hat, for fuck's sake, but thanks to your power mage hoodoo mojo bullshit, all I can think about is your dick. I got so horny while I was shopping, I rubbed one out in the dressing room. That's cuckoo fucking bananas. It's like my pussy's gone nuts. Look." She peeled the crotch of her red panties slowly aside, and Brawley saw glistening strands stretch between her sex and the lacy fabric.

"Get over here," Brawley said.

Nina put her hands on her hips and smirked, arching one eyebrow. "Look, just because I have a wet pussy, it doesn't mean you can boss me around."

"Now," Brawley said, lowering his voice.

Nina rolled her eyes but came to him. She stopped inches away and stared up at him, her gaze ticking rapidly back and forth between his eyes. Her pupils were huge, half-eclipsing her brightly mismatched irises.

"What?" she said, trying to sound tough. But he heard the quiver of desire in her voice.

Which made no sense, of course. Not with everything they'd been through. But neither did his rock-hard erection or the primal dominance rising in him.

Nina had joked about his hoodoo bullshit, but this power mage mojo was for real. It was driving them both crazy with lust.

"On your knees," he said.

Nina gasped faintly. She opened her mouth as if to speak, but Brawley stared into her eyes, and she closed her mouth and bit her lip and lowered slowly to the floor, where she knelt before him, her face inches from his crotch.

"Unzip me," he said.

Taking her time, Nina unbuckled his belt, unbuttoned his jeans, and pulled the zipper down.

Released from its denim prison, his throbbing erection jutted up mightily from the band of his jockey shorts.

Nina stared with huge eyes, peeled down his underwear, and started reaching for him.

"No touching," he said. "Not until I say so."

Nina's mouth fell open in feigned shock. "You can't tell me—"

"Hands behind your back."

Nina shook her head.

"Now."

She sighed dramatically and reached around to cross her wrists behind her lower back. "There," she said, all sassy, and arched her back, lifting her perfect tits. "Is that what you want?"

"It's what *you* want," Brawley said. "What else do you want?"

She rolled her eyes. "You know what I want."

"Say it," he told her.

"Your cock," she whispered.

"What about it?"

"I want it."

"Yes, you do. Now what did I tell you about your hands?"

Nina blushed. "Behind my back."

He nodded toward her crotch, where one of her hands had slipped inside her little red panties and was working wetly up and down. "What are you doing, then?"

"It's not fair," Nina whined. "You keep teasing me, and—"

"Behind your back."

Nina huffed with exasperation, pulled her glistening

fingers from her panties, and once more crossed her wrists behind her back just above the swell of her shapely ass.

"Open your mouth and stick out your tongue," he said.

Staring up at him, she opened her mouth and stuck out her tongue. She was trembling.

Brawley pulled himself free and held himself for her to see.

Nina's eyes swelled, and a soft moan escaped her. She leaned forward, extending her pink tongue.

Brawley made her wait.

A thin strand of drool stretched away from her straining tongue.

At the purple tip of his swollen head, a glistening bead of precum had formed. He lowered himself, barely touching the head of his erection to her tongue, then lifted it away, allowing a twinkling strand to stretch from her tongue to his tip.

Nina pulled her tongue into her mouth and groaned with a shudder. Then she opened her mouth and stuck out her tongue again. "Please."

Gripping himself by the root, Brawley slapped himself against Nina's tongue.

She strained, trying to lick him, then stretched her lips around his bulbous head.

"No sucking," he said. "Not until I say."

Her mouth popped free. Nina crossed her arms over her fantastic chest and did her best to pout.

"Stand up," he said.

Nina rose.

He frowned down at where she was playing with herself again.

She smiled nervously, pulling her hand from her panties. "Sorry. It's just I want you so bad, and—"

"Turn around."

Nina's eyes flashed with excitement. She turned and stood there with her hands at her side, swaying her perfect peach ass slowly back and forth. Her juices ran in a thin, shining line down the tanned, firm flesh of her inner thigh.

"Pull down your panties," he told her.

She complied, bracing herself against the pantry door with one arm as she stepped, still wearing her big combat boots, from the lacy twist of red fabric.

Still twitching back and forth, her ass was a study in perfection. Big, round, and firm beneath her tiny waist.

"Hands against the wall," Brawley said.

Nina leaned slightly forward and pressed her splayed fingers against the pantry door. She turned her head so that her blue eye, gleaming with lust, stared back at him through the veil of purple hair hanging from her tinfoil helmet. Her mouth was open. She was panting softly with desire, her exhalations shaking the firm flesh of her quivering body.

"Spread your legs," he said, "and stick out your ass."

Nina slid her feet apart and lowered her upper body, making the smooth muscles of her toned back ripple alluringly. She raised her ass to him. "Fill me up," she begged. "Please. My pussy has been aching for you all day."

He stepped forward and slapped his shaft crisply off her firm bottom, spanking her with his pulsing length. He felt powerful, almost euphoric, and wanted nothing in the world as much as he wanted this woman now.

With one hand, Nina clamped the foil atop her purple locks. "Just don't knock my hat off, okay?"

"Sexy," he laughed.

"Sexier than getting raided by the Order."

"Good point," he said. "You'd better hold on tight, then."

"Please," Nina begged, pushing her ass into him, trying but failing to impale herself on his massive erection. "No more teasing. Take me, Brawley. Please, take me now."

He bent his legs and inched slowly forward, sliding his shaft into the gap between her legs without touching her. Then he lifted slighting so that the length of his manhood pressed along her juicy slit from clit to crack. Without entering her, he rocked slowly back and forth, rubbing his hardness along the warm and silky folds of her sopping sex. Back and forth, back and forth, his tip grinding against the nub of her clit with every repetition.

"Uhnnn," Nina groaned, hunching and shuddering as her orgasm surprised them both. She thrust a hand between her legs, trying and failing to stop her juices as she fell forward into the wall, crying out in climax and showering the floor with her essence.

Not waiting for her to finish, Brawley slipped an arm beneath her, underhooking her lower abdomen, and pulled her still squirting sex back against him. Soaked in her juices, the head of his erection missed its mark and slid upward, trapped between them, riding the groove of her crack, the swollen head jutting up from her ass like a purple flagpole.

He shoved her hips forward, opening a gap.

"Fuck me, babe," she begged, her voice still warbling with orgasm.

Filling one hand with her perfect ass, he gripped his throbbing shaft, bent it down, and aimed the tip at her gushing mound.

He eased forward, letting his head spread her outer folds slightly, and Nina cried out again, hit by another wave of intense orgasm.

Brawley had never experienced anything this hot in his entire life. *Enough screwing around,* he thought, and was ready to plunge into her when someone started knocking frantically at the door of the RV.

Nina gave a little yelp and came away from the wall with wide eyes.

Brawley growled with frustration, swept his XDS from the table behind him, and aimed at the door, where someone was messing with the lock.

The door popped open, and Brawley rapidly turned his muzzle aside as an obviously terrified Sage rushed into the RV, an overstuffed backpack slung over one shoulder. "They're coming for us," she gasped.

"Who?" Brawley and Nina asked at the same time.

"Junior and his crew," Sage said breathlessly. "They know where we are. A technopath hacked the security cameras, I think. I had a powerful wave of foreboding and investigated, and this all came rushing in."

Brawley straightened, considering her words. And yes, there… he felt it, too. Not all the detailed stuff Sage was saying but a growing sense of doom, faint yet definite, like an ominous bell tolling over and over, growing closer with each warning strike.

"They'll be here in five minutes," Sage said. "And this time, Junior is going all out. They're looking to catch us in an ambush and kill us in one massive assault."

"Fuckshitpisscocksuckingassholes," Nina mumbled, gathering her clothes from the floor.

Sage grabbed Brawley's arm and stared up at him, her huge blue eyes pleading behind the lenses of her sexy librarian glasses. "We have to go now," she said. "We have to run before they get here. If we hurry out of town and away from the cameras, I—"

"No," Brawley said, filled with icy calm. "I won't have them on our trail. We finish this now. Here is where we make our stand."

20

"What do you mean, they're dead?" Junior said as they cruised slowly along the parking lot past the supermarket. After losing time by missing turns, they had managed to follow cameras to this shopping center. His entire crew was with him now. Rick drove. The four stone-cold killers crammed in the back of the Hummer, which bristled with weapons.

"Someone knocked out the cameras," Rick said. "This half of the lot is completely dark."

Did Nina and her boyfriend know Junior was coming? No. Almost certainly not. They were just a couple of telekinetics on the run, not a pair of Seekers.

Unless…

What if the guy was more than just Unbound?

According to Gabriella, Seekers were speculating that a new power mage might have emerged. Somewhere in the Keys, apparently. And according to Bostic, probably right here in Key West.

Whatever.

The power mages were all dead, had been since before

Junior was born, and the universe couldn't just pull a new one out of its ass. The power shift Bostic and the Seekers were sensing was Junior's rise to power, not Nina or her boyfriend, even if the asshole did end up being a power mage.

Because power mages died, too. As the Culling had proved in spades.

No, these two weren't Seekers, and they didn't know he was coming. They had simply knocked out the cameras so no one could see them sitting there.

It was a good thing, actually, proof that they were here.

The only problem now would be finding their vehicle.

And with the cameras out, that was a real problem, because neither he nor anyone in his crew was a Seeker. How the fuck would they find their vehicle even if it was still sitting here?

"There," Rick said, pointing across the dashboard, and Junior felt a rush of adrenaline.

At the far end of the lot, near the old movie theatre, sat a fancy RV. The RV itself was unfamiliar. But Junior certainly recognized the sticker-plastered pink moped leaning against the RV.

"Nina," he said, a grin stretching across his face. "Stupid mistake, girl."

He directed Rick to drive slowly past the RV. Then they looped back around the other side, keeping their distance so as not to alert Nina or her boyfriend.

The lights were on. Junior could see their silhouettes moving behind the curtains, as faint and indistinct as ghosts.

Well, soon enough they will be ghosts, he thought, and then he told Rick to pull over. Idling there, he told his men exactly what they were going to do.

His crew responded with grunts and nods and went about double-checking their weapons and ammo. These guys were pros. It had taken Junior two years of hard work to recruit them and a ridiculous amount of money keeping them on retainer. Tonight's hit alone would set him back one hundred and sixty thousand dollars, but that was a drop in the golden bucket when he looked at the big picture.

The only member of the crew showing any nerves was Rick, and he was showing plenty of nerves.

While Junior wanted as much firepower as he could muster, he knew it would be foolish to bring Rick along. The jumpy Gearhead was aces with machines but didn't have the balls for a firefight. Not even a one-sided firefight that would be over before it even started. Put a gun in Rick's hand, and he'd probably shoot his balls off.

Or my balls, Junior thought.

"Rick," Junior said, "I need you to stay here and watch the Hummer."

Rick let out a shuddering sigh. "Okay," he said. "Will do. Thanks, Junior. I really…"

Junior blocked him out, studying the lot and the RV one last time. He saw no new wrinkles, nothing to warrant questioning, let alone changing his plans.

The others were ready. None of them complained about Rick staying behind. They were paid too well to complain, of course, but Junior suspected that they were relieved to be running the hit without having to worry about friendly fire from a technopathic bundle of nerves.

For a second, he was tempted to let the pros do this alone. They could kick in the RV door and waste everyone inside. Shit, with the weapons they were carrying, they could stand outside and blast straight through the camper's walls.

But a second later, Junior rejected the notion. First of all, the plan relied on his psionics. He was going to blast a big hole straight through the RV. If Nina and her boyfriend were lucky, they would be killed instantly. If not, well they would be dead soon enough, because all four mercs would hose the interior down with hot lead.

More importantly, Junior wanted to be in on the action. He wanted to build his rep and wanted to listen to Nina and her boy toy's screams as they were blown to bits.

He would remember those screams forever. And when he took power from his father, he would replay those screams in his mind like sweet music. The soundtrack to his unstoppable success.

He'd known that he was golden once they tracked their target to the community center. Junior had grinned, watching the staticky figure embrace none other than Nina Mack.

She looked pretty staticky, too, thanks to some less powerful cloak, but he would recognize Nina anywhere. Her shape, her walk, everything.

That bitch had always acted like she was too good for Junior. It was a shame, really that he had to waste her. It would be fun to hobble her with psi-cuffs and keep her around for a while. Wear her out, then pass her to the crew as a reward. Then keep her around a little longer, just so she could see how wrong she had been to underestimate him. Ask her, after he took over as the new capo, *How do you like me now?* Then feed her fine ass to the tarpons as a nod of respect to Senior, who had, after all, paved the way and kept Junior's seat warm.

He grinned. Ever since offing that stupid Beastie that called himself the Cat Wizard, Junior had been cranked to the max, like he'd snorted a long line of crystallized psionic power. He was going to blast that RV to bits.

And yes, he would waste Nina, too. Because no piece of ass was worth risking success. Not even if she came with a side order of *I fucking told you so, bitch.*

Nope. Nina had to die. As did her boyfriend.

And their deaths would drive his power through the roof. Nina was stupid, but she was powerful, and her boyfriend clearly had big juice, based on what he did to Marco. Killing them would boost Junior to a whole new level of psionic power.

And coming so quickly on the heels of the day's earlier deaths, his wasting of these two would send a clear message to the psionic underground: do not fuck with Junior Dutchman.

Everyone would fear him. And Junior would drape their fear over his shoulders like the robe of a king.

A king who would soon ascend to his throne. Because Valdez would take note of Junior's handling of the situation. One step closer…

"We're going to strike fast and get out," Junior said. "The last thing we want is fuggle cops showing up and forcing us to waste them, too."

He'd forgotten for a second that all four of the men sitting behind him were fuggles. Not that they seemed to understand, let alone mind, the term. Their brutal faces just stared back at him, waiting to go hot.

"Kill the lights," Junior told Rick, "and pull in over there, just this side of the garbage trucks." Ever since the movie theater had gone bust, Conch Disposal had been parking their trucks here.

Rick did as he was told and pulled in behind the last truck, which put them within one hundred feet of the RV. From this range, Junior could blast the camper at full force.

"But first, you fuck up their engine, Rick," Junior said.

"Okay," the jumpy Gearhead said.

"I strike first," he reminded his soldiers.

Nods all around.

Junior was going to put all his juice into this. Blow the fucking RV to bits while the dashboard cam recorded everything. He'd have a blast later, watching his handiwork. Send a copy to Valdez, maybe. Hell, send that shit to America's Funniest Home Videos.

"I can't connect with their engine," Rick whined. He'd been twitchy as fuck for an hour. Now he seemed to be breaking down.

Junior couldn't deal with that now. It crossed his mind briefly to put a bullet through the Gearhead's brain and show the world how Junior Dutchman dealt with incompetence, but Rick was still of value to him, and besides, firing a weapon inside the Hummer would be loud as fuck and might compromise the mission.

So instead, he laid a hand on Rick's shoulder and said, "Man up, pussy. You need to hack that engine."

"I told you," Rick whined, sounding like a little bitch, "I can't. It has nothing to do with manning up. I just can't connect. It's like the RV doesn't even have an engine. It's like—"

"Shut up," Junior said, but he did his best to muzzle his rage. If you're going to lead, you have to control your emotions, even when someone deserves to die.

He turned in his seat to face the quartet of killers awaiting his orders. "All right. Fuck the engine. We're going to hit them now. Let's go."

He popped his door, grabbed the AA-12 and got out of the Hummer. With its light recoil and a drum magazine holding twenty rounds of 12 gauge ammunition, the assault shotgun was so sweet Junior almost wanted to use buckshot instead of psionics.

But that would be stupid. This wasn't just about killing his enemies. It was also about making a statement.

Once he became capo, he'd have plenty of opportunities to test the AA-12 on live targets.

His soldiers poured out of the Hummer, each carrying

one of the AK-47s Junior had acquired from his Jamaican connection. As directed, the killers paired up and moved out in opposite directions without so much as a whisper.

One pair took up position twenty yards from the front of the RV and crouched down behind a compact car. The other pair jogged to the closest garbage truck and trained their weapons on the rear of the camper. At that range, the armor-piercing rounds would punch through the ass end of the RV, blow through the center, and blast out the headlights.

Junior drew his strand, build energy for several seconds before shaping a tight bolt of sizzling force that would blow the camper wide open. He grinned, loving the boost he'd received from killing the Cat Wizard. This was sweet.

Shit, now he wished he had killed Marco himself, since the guy was slated for death anyway. Oh well. Too late now. He had the rest of his life to kill psi mages.

Starting with Nina Mack and her asshole boyfriend.

Catching the attention of his men, Junior raised three fingers in the air, folding them as he counted down silently.

3… 2… 1…

Junior struck.

The force of the attack snapped his head back as the bolt whipped from his mind, shot straight as a rocket, and hit the RV broadside. There was a loud clang and an explosion of fiery sparks. Twisted, flaming wreckage tumbled loudly away as the AKs lit up, muzzle flashes strobing to techno beat of high-caliber weapons firing full auto.

The demolished RV rolled to a stop twenty feet away and lay on its side, sparking as the 7.62 rounds panged loudly, punching holes in the undercarriage.

Only that wasn't an undercarriage, Junior realized three seconds into the attack.

No, not an undercarriage. And not an RV. Not at all.

As the men swapped out mags and advanced on the thing, firing, Junior saw the truth.

Lying on its side, blasted into a smoking twist of metal pocked with dozens of bullet holes, was not an RV but a dumpster.

There was no RV, no moped, no Nina, no boyfriend.

It had all been an illusion. Some kind of Seeker illusion cloaking the dumpster.

Not just an illusion, but…

A roar sounded from the other side of the garbage trucks, and a dark shape lurched from the shadows where it had been hiding.

A fucking trap.

The onrushing RV's lights clicked on like the eyes of some great monster, blinding the nearest pair of shooters, who had just enough time to shout before the RV slammed into them. There was a loud thump, and the two mercs skipped and skittered across the lot in tumbling bundles of dead meat.

Their deaths bought the other two men a second of reaction time. One threw down his empty AK, drew a sidearm, and fired two rounds at the driver, shattering the windshield before a wall of invisible force slammed into him and punted him forty feet across the lot. The man struck the pavement and bounced, his entire body flopping in too many directions at once, having apparently developed two or three hinges along his broken spine.

The last soldier dove for cover behind the car, which the RV struck with a loud thump and another spray of sparks. Then a moped whined out of the darkness, cutting across the dim lot at an angle. Whipping past the remaining soldier, Nina raised her arm. A fireworks display of muzzle flashes blossomed in the gloom, and Nina filled the night with a sound Junior recognized as the buzz saw of Miguel's Mac-10.

His only remaining soldier cried out sharply, and the man's silhouette did a gruesome moonwalk across the pavement, jerking and lurching and stumbling backwards as a barrage of heavy rounds punched him full of holes. A second later, he was down, dead as a spent casing, and Junior was alone.

No. Not alone. Rick was still...

But Junior heard the squeal of tires and roar of the Hummer's engine, and understood that no, he had been right. He was alone. Rick, being the fucking coward he was, had bolted like a frightened rabbit.

Should've killed the son of a bitch when I had the chance, Junior thought. Oh well. He'd just have to kill the cowardly fuck later.

Right now, he had to finish this shit and seize his destiny. Tonight, the power shifted.

He wished he had psi power left, but he'd wasted it on the fucking dumpster.

Even as he had these thoughts, even as he registered Rick's betrayal, Junior raised the shotgun to his shoulder, tracking the pink moped.

Unfortunately, Nina never slowed. She just blasted his merc and kept flying away. In a second, she would be long gone.

Junior found her with his sights and pulled the trigger. But even as the shotgun boomed, kicking him in the shoulder, Junior registered the metal wall appearing between his muzzle flash and the disappearing girl.

The RV had lurched backwards, giving the escaping moped cover and blocking his shot. Son of a bitch!

And now...

His heart lurched.

What the fuck?

The RV door swung open. The crazy bastard was sprinting straight at him.

And not just any crazy bastard, Junior realized, his mind racing with adrenaline. It was that dumb ass who'd saved the cat at Mallory Square.

Junior swung the barrel in that direction, but twin blossoms of fire bloomed before the charging silhouette. Two gunshots sounded, one atop the other, and son of a bitch!

Something punched Junior in the hip so hard that his legs kicked out from beneath him. His upper body slammed to the ground hard, the shotgun smacking into the pavement and discharging at a weird angle. Adding insult to injury, the accidental discharge hurt like a bastard, yanking his unprepared wrist at an awkward angle even as his face smashed into the jerking barrel.

Holy fuck, he thought as a volcano of pain exploded in his hip, radiating across his pelvis and pulsing down his thighs and up into his gut. *I'm shot. That crazy fucker shot me.*

He realized then that two more shots had rung out as he dropped, the rounds cutting the air over his head.

Lucky, that.

Clutching the shotgun to his chest, Junior rolled to his right behind the trash truck where he lay on his belly, sighting down the barrel, scanning the lot.

There!

He fired just as the asshole dove behind a car. Then fired again, holding the trigger for an instant, firing three-four-five times, peppering the car with buckshot, smashing out its windows, and hopefully killing the son of a bitch who'd shot him.

Goddamn, getting shot hurt!

He tried to stand, but his hip and leg were all fucked up. His back, too. There wasn't much pain there, strangely enough. More in his gut and nuts and upper leg, but it felt like his hip and pelvis and lower back had all come undone.

So be it. So fucking be it. He would deal with that soon enough. But first he had to lay here and wait for this crazy son of a bitch to pop up and give him another shot.

At this range, lying prone, he couldn't miss.

21

Brawley hunkered down behind the car, weighing his options. When he'd leapt from the RV, he'd planned to finish it there and then, but Junior—and his gut told him that yes, it was Junior—had opened up with a scattergun.

Brawley had taken a pellet or two to the upper arm before diving behind the car. His shoulder throbbed, and warm blood was running down his arm, but he believed the pellets had passed clean through the meat, and he had full motion in the arm, so he wasn't going to worry about that. Pain was just pain. As he had countless times over his life, Brawley told the pain to go fuck itself and kept on riding.

He had hit Junior at least once and put him down, but he hadn't killed the prick, a fact that became crystal clear when the shotgun started blasting away. The car shuddered, and glass rained down on Brawley, who was, luckily enough, crouched down on the other side of a cement divider. Otherwise, Junior's buckshot might've punched a mess of holes through Brawley's boots and feet.

If only the son of a bitch had been carrying one of those big ass AKs instead of a shotgun.

As is, Brawley couldn't rush him. Buckshot was indiscriminate. It didn't care if a target was a psychotic asshole or a good dude just trying to protect his women. At twenty-some yards, one blast would blow Brawley in half.

So he couldn't rush Junior. What choice did that leave him?

Maybe the son of a bitch was bleeding out over there.

It wasn't a thing to take for granted.

Brawley popped up quickly, saw the flash, and dropped back down without even trying to take a shot. He heard the heavy whump of the shotgun, and buckshot slammed into the car, which lurched and sighed, a rear tire going flat.

In the distance, sirens were wailing.

No matter how long I live, I will never again think of Key West without remembering the sound of wailing sirens. In his mind, the cry of approaching sirens were as much a part of this place as the whine of windmills was part of his life back on the ranch.

Only windmills whining, unlike these sirens, didn't mean people were coming to either shoot your ass or throw you in jail.

And yet those distant sirens didn't really concern Brawley.

The noise that concerned him was coming from the other direction. A soft whine, buzzing closer.

Nina was coming back. She was flying this way. He had told her to stay away, explaining that he would pick her up with Sage later, but she was coming back to stand beside him.

Which meant he had to finish this now.

He still had a little bit of telekinetic juice left, enough to bloody Junior's nose or maybe even to knock him out, but he would need a clear line of sight to do that. He'd be faster and better off with a pistol.

But he was pinned down.

What could he do?

Think!

What about his Seeker juice? According to the girls, power mages of old learned to splice their powers. The strongest among them could lend psi power from one strand to another, creating emergency fuel or even supercharging an action by doubling the energy behind it.

But Brawley had no clue how to even try that.

For now, his Seeker energy remained just that, Seeker energy, not a flexible reserve of force he could weaponize.

The only thing he'd managed, under Sage's direction, to do with Seeker force was to create the illusory carbon copy of Nina's moped.

What he needed now from his Seeker energy was information. He needed to know what to do.

He reached out with his mind. He didn't even know how to connect with the Latticework, let alone what to do if he actually managed to connect. So instead he just reached out with his mind, focusing his thoughts on Junior and the problem at hand.

He felt a dull warmth at the center of his mind and suddenly knew, beyond a shadow of a doubt, that Junior was lying behind the last garbage truck, hidden behind the far side, just the other side of the tire. Junior was hurt bad, shot through the hip and bleeding pretty good, but he was still fully conscious. In a minute or two, Brawley's intuition told him, Junior would likely slide into shock or pass out from blood loss.

But Brawley didn't have that much time, because the buzzing whine of Nina's moped was coming closer, cutting through the lot and hurrying this way. She'd be here in twenty seconds.

And Junior was just lying there, waiting to pull the trigger. It didn't matter to him whether he blasted Brawley or Nina.

Brawley had to finish this shit right now.

If only Nina wasn't really Nina. If only she was an illusion, approaching on an illusory moped like the one Brawley had made earlier.

What if...

The whine of Nina's moped drew closer. She was fifteen seconds from shotgun range.

Brawley had to try.

Remembering Sage's instruction, he focused his mind and drew the buzzing yellow Seeker energy together, shaping it as quickly as he could, infusing it with false truth, and setting his construction in motion.

He felt the whoosh of force leave his mind, but he wasn't sure the action had worked and wasn't sure how long it had taken, but the buzz of Nina's moped was much closer now, and he heard her sweet voice calling out his name.

At the same second, he jumped to his feet, going for broke, and sprinted out from behind the car, raising his XDS.

Junior's shotgun roared—*boom-boom-boom-boom-boom*—flashing brightly in the gathering gloom, blasting the long, tall Texan sprinting in his direction.

Brawley's mirror image wavered and faded as the buckshot punched straight through the empty air into which it was disappearing.

Brawley's illusory twin had lasted only two seconds, but it was enough.

Meanwhile, the real Brawley, having come around the other side of the car, angled around the garbage truck, spotted Junior firing away on the ground, and fired his XDS.

Junior's body jerked with impact.

Brawley stopped running, steadied his aim, and took four measured shots before holstering his XDS and pulling the Sigma 9.

All of his shots had struck Junior. He'd seen the son of a bitch jerk and roll and jerk again like a jig at the end of a fishing line.

Brawley advanced slowly, training the 9mm on the twitching silhouette, and reached out with his mind to see what he could see.

Junior was dead, his Seeker brain told him. All gone save for a few last death twitches.

From five yards away, Brawley still pulled the trigger. Junior's body jerked again. This time, the shadowy knob of his skull went to pieces, spraying across the shadowy ground in a dark smear.

Sure, his Seeker force had told him Junior was dead. But Brawley still approached from behind. He wasn't ready to bet his survival on Seeker info, not when he had a simpler option.

Better safe than sorry, he thought, stepping close and pulling the trigger one more time. *And there's no wiggle room in a headshot.*

22

Brawley drove slowly, leaning at an awkward angle to see through the small section of windshield not spiderwebbed by bullet holes.

"Focus on the road," Sage suggested from the passenger seat, "and you will be able to feel the truth of it without needing to see."

"Maybe next time," Brawley said. "For right now, I'll just play it safe and go old school."

"*Keep your hands on the wheel and your eyes upon the road,*" Nina sang from where she stood just behind them, one hand resting on each of their head rests.

"Hey," Brawley said. "You have a pretty voice."

"You're just trying to sweet-talk me so you can get me into your Murphy bed back there."

"I mean what I say and say what I mean. You really do have a nice voice." Brawley squinted as a set of headlights passed on the other side of Route 1. "But yeah, once we get up the road a ways, I am going to pull this thing over and fuck both of you."

Nina snorted dubiously. "Don't make any promises you can't keep."

"I always keep my promises, darlin."

When Brawley was six or seven years old, his grandmother had told him that all cowboys wanted to do two things before they died: kill a bad man and love a good woman.

Today, Brawley had killed nine and loved two. More killing lay ahead. But first, he'd enjoy the loving, which he planned to make the most of.

"And I do mean both of you," he clarified, "at the same time."

The girls looked at each other.

Sage twitched her glasses up the bridge of her nose and smiled.

Nina, on the other hand, blushed. Glancing at her blond friend, she squirmed. Maybe nervous, maybe eager. Maybe both.

"If we bond, we bond," Brawley said. "Shit's about to get real."

"Um, we're on the run after killing a bunch of people," Nina said, "including Junior Dutchman. I think it's safe to say shit already got real."

"I am eager to feel your penis inside me again, Master," Sage said.

"Oh brother," Nina said. "Don't encourage him, or his head will get so big, we'll need another RV just to carry it."

Brawley laughed.

"It is only natural the we feel submissive to our psi-husband," Sage explained. "After all, he is a—"

"I know, I know," Nina interrupted. "He's a power mage. Please stop reminding him. And chill on the husband stuff. Can't he just be our psi-guy or power dude or something?"

"It doesn't matter what you call me," Brawley said. "We're bound. I'm going to love and protect you both forever."

"That makes me very happy," Nina said. She leaned in and kissed his cheek. "And I will love and protect you—both of you—for the rest of my life."

Brawley grinned at her.

"What?" Nina said. "I mean it."

"I know you do," he said. "It's just hard to take you seriously when you're wearing that crazy hat."

"Aargh," Nina said, clapping a hand over the tinfoil helmet, which remained in place due to the rubber band that Sage had stretched over the foil and under Nina's chin before the big fight with Junior and his crew.

They hadn't talked much about what had happened back there. Maybe they would later. Or maybe they wouldn't.

Brawley didn't need to talk. He already knew how he felt about it. They had killed five assholes who had tried to kill them. Simple math there. His only regret was not being able to kill the one who'd abandoned Junior.

In time, he thought. *In time.*

Because he was certain that he hadn't seen the last of the psi mafia.

Or the Order.

Or a whole shit ton of other people who were coming for him now, just like Hazel said they would.

Which all led to the same conclusion: Miami. And that was going to be a game changer. Big time.

They had escaped Key West just in time. They'd only had time to scoop up two AKs, two bandoliers of AK magazines, and Junior's assault shotgun. By the time they had thrown them into the RV and lifted Nina's moped through the door, they could see the flashing lights of the first police cars arriving at the far end of the sprawling shopping center.

They had driven behind the last strip of shops and picked

up Sage, who cloaked them in darkness until they reached the end of the island. Then Sage had shifted the illusion, simply changing the color of the RV and giving onlookers the sense that the windshield was still in one piece.

"Get me to Marathon so I can get a mind shield and ditch this stupid hat," Nina said.

"I don't know," Brawley said, showing her a cockeyed grin. "I'm getting kind of attached to it."

Sage laughed from the passenger seat. "A falsehood. Humorous in its juxtaposition to Nina's ridiculous appearance."

Nina feigned shock. *"Nina's ridiculous appearance?* The fuck, girlfriend? I thought we were tight. Besides," she said, and struck a sexy pose, "I make tinfoil look hot."

Their laughter cut off when they rounded the corner and saw a wall of flashing lights stretching across the highway on both sides.

Another roadblock.

Brawley slowed to a stop behind the line of cars waiting to be checked.

"You still good, girlfriend?" Nina asked.

"Yes," Sage said with a bright smile. "Just this morning, I never would have possessed the energy to do everything I've done, let alone to still feel this powerful."

"Excellent," Brawley said. He, too, felt powerful. Killing Junior had given him a boost just like killing Marco had. "And soon, you'll be even more powerful."

"Is that your Seeker side spitting prophecies," Nina asked, "or an awkward segue into a confession about plans for adding women?"

"These people aren't going to stop hunting me," Brawley said, easing the RV forward as another car passed through the roadblock. "The psi mafia, the Order, the fuggle cops, those government types you mentioned."

"The FPI," Nina said with a shudder. "Once they catch your scent, they will pour everything into hunting you."

"While this truth distresses me," Sage said, "you are correct, husband. Everyone will soon be chasing you. Those you have mentioned, all seven Orders, and a good portion of the Chaotics, as well. Across the Latticework, opinions are coalescing around the belief that a new power mage has arisen in Key West. Even now, various factions are heading this way from across the globe. Some will attempt to kill you. Others wish to study you. Many want to render you for energy."

"Some of them want to use you," Nina sang.

Brawley eased the RV forward. Just ahead, cops were poking around cars, examining interiors with flashlights. Brawley felt a flicker of unease, imagining the policemen coming onboard the RV, but then he squashed it. In for a penny, in for a pound. And he was in for the pound. Every last fucking ounce.

"I'm going all in," he said. "I'm going to open all seven strands and become a true power mage. And with every strand I open, you two will become more powerful, too."

"I must say that power is intoxicating," Sage said. "I, for one, support this plan. It is the only logical way to proceed, so long as we are able to find five suitable teachers for you."

"Are you kidding me?" Nina said. "He's a handsome cowboy with a nice ass, a big dick, and oh yeah... he's a fucking power mage. I might not be a Seeker, but I'll tell you right now, our guy will have no trouble scoring psi-babes."

"This shit is forever, though," Brawley said, "so I'm not going to bond with just anybody."

"Oh boy," Nina said, "we're in the company of a diva."

"Our husband is wise to be discerning," Sage said. "The bonds of a power mage are, indeed, everlasting. None of us wishes to be paired for eternity with a bad fit. And as you expressed, Nina, women will seek our husband. We must be very cautious in selecting our sister-wives."

Brawley laughed. This was surreal as fuck. Doubly so because they were inching ever closer to a roadblock manned by heavily armed police officers. "*We* have to be cautious? I'll be choosing my wives, not you."

"Chill with the wife thing," Nina said, giving his uninjured shoulder a squeeze. "And we obviously get a say in whom you choose."

"If you girls want to help me recruit women, that's fine," Brawley said, "but I already know which strand I'm opening next. We're heading for Miami."

"I thought we were headed for Texas."

"Eventually," he said, "but you girls said South Beach is Carnal Central, right?"

They nodded.

"Well, getting shot doesn't tickle," he said. A piece of buckshot had blown clean through his shoulder, leaving the back of his arm swollen and purple. "And I got a feeling people aren't done trying to shoot me."

"You're going to bond with a Carnal?" Nina said.

"I am," Brawley said. "You don't sound thrilled. I thought you wanted me to open more strands."

"I do," Nina said, "but ugh… I hate Carnals. They're all hot and cocky and full of themselves. Why not start with someone else? I know a nice Beastie girl. She's sweet as pie and super hot. You'd love her."

"I'm sure I will," Brawley said, "but first, I need regeneration, so we're heading to Miami."

"Fuck me Freddy," Nina said. "This is all so goddamned crazy. Buckle in, Sage. We are in for a rough ride."

"Rough rides are the only ones worth taking," Brawley said. "You can't score 90 points on a timid bull."

"Don't go muddling shit with your bull riding allusions," Nina said. "Hey, fuzz at ten o'clock."

The officer reached up and rapped on Brawley's window with his flashlight. A peel of unintelligible chatter squawked from the walkie-talkie at his hip.

Brawley rolled down his window.

"I'm sorry to bother you, ma'am," the police officer said.

Brawley grinned.

Ma'am.

So Sage did have a sense of humor. He just hoped that Sage had manipulated his voice, too, or this cop was in for a shock. "What's the problem, officer?"

"I can't say much, ma'am," the officer said, offering a polite frown, "but there was an incident in Key West tonight, and suspects fled the scene. We're stopping all vehicles to make sure they don't slip by. Would you mind if I took a quick look inside your vehicle?"

Sage leaned past Brawley and smiled at the cop. "Hello, officer. We are not the people you are looking for."

The policeman nodded.

"But please do shine your flashlight around inside our vehicle," Sage said.

"Yes, ma'am," the cop said, and swept his light back and forth. Settling its beam on Nina, he said, "Sir, I'm going to have to ask you to sit down and fasten your seat belt."

It was all Brawley could do not to burst out laughing. *Sage, you mischievous little Seeker.*

"Sorry, officer," Nina said, taking a seat and pulling the shoulder belt across her body.

"That's okay, sir," the policeman said. "Sorry to trouble you folks. You all have a nice night."

"Thanks," Brawley said, and rolled through the stop point.

Route 1 was the only road back to the mainland, a

hundred-mile stretch of bridges and highway flanked on both sides by island towns and breathtaking ocean views.

Now, however, darkness was upon them, and up ahead, enemies were getting into position, transforming this world-famous scenic drive into a deadly gauntlet.

A rough ride indeed.

So be it. Brawley was ready.

"Sir?" Nina said incredulously as they picked up speed. "What the shit was that, Sage? You made me look like a man, didn't you?" The seat belt stretched tightly across Nina's body, pulling the skimpy half shirt down between her breasts and exposing the edge of her red bra, the swell of her incredible curves, and shadowy hollows of her alluring collarbones.

And wouldn't you fucking know it, Brawley had iron in his pants again.

Seeing a turnoff ahead, he hit the blinker.

There was a time to kill and a time to fuck, and he'd killed enough people for one day.

They would stop, have some fun, and rest, which power all three of them up to max juice again.

And God have mercy on anyone who tried to stop them.

———

THANK YOU FOR READING *POWER MAGE!*

If you enjoyed the book, please be awesome and leave a review. When you leave a review, even a short one, Amazon shows my book to more people. Thanks for your time and help.

Brawley's adventures continue in *Power Mage 2.* Are you ready for more power, more problems, and more women?

Get your barbaric ass on my mailing list.

Speaking of savages, special thanks to Tanner Likins,

whose feedback on an advance copy made this a better book. The first beer is on me, dude.

Check out the Harem Lit Facebook group, where fans of the genre hang out and talk books. I look forward to meeting you there.

Until then, don't approach a bull from the front, a horse from the rear, or a fool from any direction.

ALSO BY HONDO JINX

Power Mage

Power Mage 2

Power Mage 3

Dan the Barbarian

Dan the Adventurer

Dan the Destroyer

Dan the Warlord

Together, the Dan books complete GOLD, GIRLS, AND GLORY, an epic four-book fantasy adventure series.

Cut class. Kick ass. Save the frigging world.

When Dan's life blends with a tabletop RPG adventure, he grabs his talking two-handed sword and hits campus looking for girls, gold, and glory. Join Dan as he transforms from a half-stepping college student into a savage warlord who drinks from the skulls of his enemies.

Warning: This series is intended for readers 18 and older. It includes explicit sex, profanity, graphic violence, and a harem of gorgeous ass-kicking women.

WITHDRAWN

CPSIA information can be obtained
at www.ICGtesting.com
Printed in the USA
LVHW102357031122
732309LV00004B/406

9 781084 195530